THE BOOK OF MURDER

THE BOOK OF MURDER

Guillermo Martínez

*Translated from Spanish
by Sonia Soto*

VIKING

VIKING
Published by the Penguin Group
Penguin Group (USA) Inc., 375 Hudson Street,
New York, New York 10014, U.S.A.
Penguin Group (Canada), 90 Eglinton Avenue East, Suite 700,
Toronto, Ontario, Canada M4P 2Y3
(a division of Pearson Penguin Canada Inc.)
Penguin Books Ltd, 80 Strand, London WC2R 0RL, England
Penguin Ireland, 25 St. Stephen's Green, Dublin 2, Ireland
(a division of Penguin Books Ltd)
Penguin Books Australia Ltd, 250 Camberwell Road, Camberwell,
Victoria 3124, Australia
(a division of Pearson Australia Group Pty Ltd)
Penguin Books India Pvt Ltd, 11 Community Centre, Panchsheel Park,
New Delhi - 110 017, India
Penguin Group (NZ), 67 Apollo Drive, Rosedale, North Shore 0632,
New Zealand (a division of Pearson New Zealand Ltd)
Penguin Books (South Africa) (Pty) Ltd, 24 Sturdee Avenue,
Rosebank, Johannesburg 2196, South Africa

Penguin Books Ltd, Registered Offices:
80 Strand, London WC2R 0RL, England

First American edition
Published in 2008 by Viking Penguin,
a member of Penguin Group (USA) Inc.

1 3 5 7 9 10 8 6 4 2

Originally published in Spanish under the title *La muerte lenta de Luciana B.* by Ediciones Destino, Barcelona. English translation first published in Great Britain by Abacus, an imprint of Little, Brown Book Group.

Publisher's Note
This is a work of fiction. Names, characters, places, and incidents either are the product of the author's imagination or are used fictitiously, and any resemblance to actual persons, living or dead, business establishments, events, or locales is entirely coincidental.

LIBRARY OF CONGRESS CATALOGING IN PUBLICATION DATA

Martínez, Guillermo, 1962-
[Muerte lenta de Luciana B. English]
The book of murder / Guillermo Martínez ; translated from Spanish by Sonia Soto.
p. cm.
ISBN 978-0-670-01994-6
I. Soto, Sonia. II. Title.
PQ7798.23.A69165M8413 2008
863'.7—dc22
2008015564

Printed in the United States of America

Tout ce qui heurte en physique souffre le même choc de la réaction; mais en morale la réaction est plus forte de l'action. La réaction de l'imposture est le mépris; celle du mépris est la haine; celle de la haine est l'homicide.

In the physical world anything which strikes is subjected to the same force in reaction; but in the moral world the reaction is stronger than the action. The reaction from being imposed upon is scorn; the reaction from scorn is hatred; the reaction from hatred is murder.

Giacomo Casanova, *The Story of My Life*

1

The telephone rang one Sunday morning, tearing me from the sleep of the dead. When I answered, a voice simply said *Luciana*, in a weak, anxious whisper, as if it were all I'd need to remember her. Disconcerted, I echoed the name, and she added her surname, which roused a distant memory. Then, in an anguished tone, she reminded me who she was: Luciana B, the girl who took dictation. Of course I remembered. Had it really been ten years? Yes, almost ten, she confirmed. She was glad I still lived in the same flat. But she didn't sound at all glad. She paused. Could she see me? She *had* to see me, she corrected herself, the desperation in her voice removing any possible delusions on my part.

'Yes, of course,' I said, slightly alarmed. 'When?'

'Whenever you can, as soon as possible.'

I looked round doubtfully at my untidy flat, testament to the indolent forces of entropy, and glanced at the clock on the bedside table. 'If it's a matter of life and death,' I said, 'what about this afternoon, here, say at four?'

There was a hoarse sound at the other end of the line and a faltering breath, as if she were trying to hold back a sob. 'I'm sorry,' she mumbled, embarrassed. 'Yes, it is a matter of life and death. You really don't know, do you? Nobody knows. Nobody *realises*.' I thought she was about to cry again. There was a silence, during which she struggled to regain her composure. Even more quietly, as if she could hardly bring herself to say the name, she whispered: 'It's about Kloster.' And before I could ask any questions, as if afraid I might change my mind, she said: 'I'll be there at four.'

Ten years earlier, I had broken my right wrist in a stupid accident and had gone about with my hand, to the tips of my fingers, held in the rigid grip of a plaster cast. At the time, I was due to deliver my second novel to the publisher but all I had was a draft in my impossible handwriting – two thick spiral notebooks riddled with deletions, arrows and corrections that no one but me could decipher. After thinking it over for a few moments, my editor, Campari, came up with the solution: he knew that Kloster had for some time now been using a typist –

a girl, very young and apparently so perfect in every way that she had become one of his most prized possessions.

'So why would he lend her to me?' I asked, afraid to believe my luck. Kloster's name, plucked from on high and dropped so casually by Campari, had impressed me a little despite myself. We were in Campari's office and a framed copy of the dust jacket of Kloster's first novel that hung on the wall – the editor's only concession to decoration – created a resonance that was hard to ignore.

'I'm sure he wouldn't want to. But Kloster's out of the country till the end of the month. He's at one of those writers' retreats where he shuts himself away to polish his novels before publication. He hasn't taken his wife with him, so by extension,' he said with a wink, 'I shouldn't think his wife has let him take his secretary.'

There and then he called Kloster's home, offered effusive greetings to someone who was evidently the wife, listened with resignation to what must have been a list of complaints, waited patiently for her to find the name in the address book, and at last jotted down a number on a slip of paper.

'The girl's called Luciana,' he said. 'But be careful. You know Kloster's the jewel in our crown – you've got to return her intact at the end of the month.'

The conversation, though brief, had provided a glimpse into the very private, reclusive existence of the only truly quiet writer in a country whose authors liked above all to talk. As I'd listened to Campari I'd grown more and more surprised and couldn't help voicing my thoughts: Kloster, the terrible Kloster, had a wife? He even had something as unthinkable, as positively bourgeois, as a secretary?

'And a little girl he adores,' added Campari. 'He was almost forty when she was born. I've bumped into him a couple of times when he's been taking her to the park. Yes, he's a loving family man. Who'd have thought it?'

At any rate, although sales of Kloster's books hadn't yet exploded, as they later would, he had for some time, particularly since the publication of his tetralogy, been the writer we all wanted to destroy. Since his first book, he'd been too big, too good. Between novels, he withdrew into bewildering silence, which we found unsettling, threatening: it was the silence of the cat while the mice published their efforts. With each new ground-breaking work, we wondered not how he'd done it but how he'd *done it again*. And to make matters worse, he wasn't even as old, as far removed from our generation, as we'd have liked. We comforted ourselves with the thought that Kloster must be from another species, a malevolent freak, rejected by humanity, shut away, resentful and alone, as hideous in appearance as any of his characters. We imagined that before becoming a writer he had been a forensic pathologist, or museum embalmer, or hearse driver. After all, he had chosen as the epigraph for one of his books the contemptuous words of Kafka's 'hunger artist': 'I had to fast because I couldn't find a food I enjoyed. If I had found that I would have eaten to my heart's content.'

On the back cover of his first book it said politely that there was something 'unholy' about his observations, but as soon as you started reading his work it became clear that Kloster wasn't unholy, he was merciless. From the opening paragraphs, his novels dazzled, like the head-lights of a car on the road, and too late you realised that you'd become the terrified rabbit, frozen, heart beating, and all you could do was continue, hypnotically, to turn the pages. There was something almost physical, and cruel, in the way his stories pierced layers, stirring long-buried fears, as if Kloster had the sinister gift of boring into your brain while holding you down with the subtlest of pincers. Nor were they exactly, reassuringly, *detective stories* (how we would have liked to dismiss him as the author of mere detective stories). What there was in them was evil, in its purest form. And if the word hadn't been so overused and devalued by TV soaps it might have pro-vided the best definition of his novels: they were *evil*. Proof of how he loomed over us like a colossus was the way we spoke of him in hushed tones, as if nobody 'out-side' would find out about him if we strove to keep him secret. Nor did the critics really know how to deal with him, and all they could do was stammer that Kloster wrote 'too' well, so as to seem unimpressed. And they were right: he did write too well. Out of reach. In every scene, every line of dialogue, every finishing touch, the lesson was the same – and discouraging. I'd tried a hundred times to 'see' how he did it, but I'd concluded simply that behind the desk there must be an obsessive, magnificently sick mind with the power of life and death, a barely restrained megalomaniac. So it's hardly surprising that ten years ago I was absolutely fascinated by the prospect of seeing what the 'perfect' secretary of this fanatical perfectionist was like.

I phoned her – a calm, cheerful, polite voice – as soon as I got back to my flat, and we arranged to meet. When I went down to let her in I found a tall, slim girl, with a serious yet smiling face, high forehead, brown hair drawn back into a ponytail. Attractive? Very attractive, and terribly young – she looked like a first-year student, just out of the shower. Jeans and a loose blouse, coloured wristbands on one wrist, trainers with a star print. We smiled at each other without speaking in the narrow confines of the lift: very white, even teeth, hair still a little damp at the ends, scent . . . Inside my apartment, we soon agreed hours and pay. She sat down quite casually at the computer, dropping her small handbag beside her, and making the chair swivel gently with her long legs as we talked. Brown eyes, an intelligent, quick, sometimes cheerful look. A serious yet smiling face.

That first day she took dictation for two straight hours. She was fast, sure and, as an added miracle, made no spelling mistakes. Her hands on the keyboard hardly seemed to move. She adapted straight away to my voice and pace, and never lost the thread. Perfect, then, in every way? At almost thirty, I was starting to look with cruel melancholy into women's futures and I couldn't help noticing other things about her. Her hair, starting high on her forehead, was very fine and brittle and if you looked down on her from above (I dictated standing up), her parting was a little too wide. Also her jawline was not as firm as one might have wished, a slight fleshiness at her throat threatening in time to become a double chin. And before she sat down I noticed that from the waist down she suffered from the characteristic Argentinian asymmetry, as yet only incipient, of excessive hips. But all this lay far in the future, and for now her youth overcame any flaws.

As I opened the first notebook to begin dictating, she straightened her back in the chair and I confirmed, with disappointment, what I had suspected: her blouse fell straight over a completely flat chest. But might this not have been a convenient defence for Kloster, perhaps a decisive one? As I had recently found out, Kloster was married, and he would have had trouble introducing an eighteen-year-old nymphet to his wife if the girl had generous curves as well. But above all, if the writer wanted to work undistracted, wasn't it a perfect arrangement? He had the youthful grace of her profile, which he could calmly admire while he worked, whilst avoiding any sexual tension that might have come from another, more dangerous contour? I wondered if Kloster had made this kind of calculation, this kind of secret deliberation. I wondered – as Pessoa had – if it was only I who was so vile, 'vile in the literal sense of the word'. In any case, I approved of his choice.

At one point I suggested we have coffee. Displaying the same self-assurance with which she had made herself at home, she stood and, pointing at the plaster cast on my hand, said she'd make it if I told her where everything was. She mentioned that Kloster drank coffee constantly (actually, she didn't say Kloster, she used his first name, and I wondered how close they had become) and that the first thing he'd done was instruct her how to make it. That first day I didn't ask anything more about Kloster, because I was sufficiently intrigued by him to be able to wait until she and I had got to know each other better, but I did find out, as she gathered cups and saucers in the kitchen, almost everything I would ever know about Luciana. She was indeed at university, in her first year. She was studying biology but was thinking of changing subject. Mummy, daddy, an older brother in his final year of medicine, a much younger sister, aged seven, mentioned with an ambivalent smile, as if she were an endearing pest. A grandmother who'd been in an old people's home for some time. A boyfriend discreetly slipped into the conversation, without actually mentioning his name, with whom she'd been going out for a year. Had she slept with the boyfriend? I made a few cynical remarks and she laughed. I decided she had, definitely. She'd studied ballet but given it up when she began at university, although she had retained the upright posture and something of the outward turn of the feet when standing. She'd been to England, on an exchange – with a grant from her bilingual school. In short, I reflected at the time, a proud expensive daughter, a finished example, perfectly educated and polished, of Argentina's middle class, seeking work much earlier than her friends. I wondered, but didn't ask, why quite so early, but maybe it was simply a sign of her apparent maturity and independence. She really didn't look as if she needed the small sum we'd agreed: she was still tanned from a long summer at the house by the sea that her parents owned in Villa Gesell, and her tiny handbag alone must have cost more than my old computer on the desk in front of her.

She took dictation for a couple of hours more and only once did she show any sign of tiredness: during a pause she bent her head to one side, then the other, and her neck, her pretty neck, made a sharp crack. When her time was up, she stood, collected the coffee cups, washed them up and left them to drain by the sink. She gave me a quick kiss on the cheek and left.

And this was the pattern from then on: a kiss on arrival, her little bag dropped, almost thrown, beside the sofa, two hours of dictation, coffee and a brief, smiling conversation in the narrow kitchen, two more hours' work, and at a certain point, unfailingly, the bending of her head to one side then the other, half painfully, half seductively, and the sharp crack of her vertebrae. I got to know her clothes, the changes in her face – sometimes more sleepy than others – the variations in hairstyle, the coded signals of her make-up. At one point I did ask about Kloster, but by that time I was much more interested in her than in him. She had indeed started to seem to me perfect in every way, and I was dreaming up improbable scenarios in which I kept her working for me. But Kloster, apparently, was perfect in every way as a boss. He was considerate, giving her time off for exams, and she let me know, tactfully, that he paid her almost double what she'd agreed with me. But what was the man like, the mysterious Mr K, I insisted. What did I want to know? she asked, disconcerted. *Everything*, of course. Didn't she know that we writers were professional gossips? No one knew him, I explained; he didn't give interviews and photos of him hadn't appeared with his books for a long time now. She looked surprised. It was true, she'd heard him turn down interviews several times, but she'd never imagined there could be anything mysterious about him: he didn't appear to have any secrets. He must have been a little over forty, was tall and slim; in his youth he'd been a long-distance swimmer, there were cups and medals from that time in his study, and he sometimes still went swimming late at night at a club near his house.

She'd carefully chosen the few words she used to describe him, as if she wanted to make sure she sounded neutral, and I wondered if she was interested in him in any way. So he was tall, slim, with broad swimmer's shoulders, I summed up. Attractive? I fired the word at her. She laughed, as if she'd already considered and discounted it: 'No, at least not to me.' And she added, sounding a little shocked: 'He's old enough to be my father.' And anyway, she said, he was *very* serious. They too worked for four hours every morning. He had a lovely little girl, four years old, who was always drawing pictures for Luciana and would have liked her for a big sister. The daughter played on her own in a room on the ground floor next to the study while they worked. His wife never appeared – Luciana did find this a little mysterious. She'd only ever seen her a couple of times. Sometimes she heard her shouting something at the little girl, or calling her from upstairs. Maybe she was a depressive, or perhaps she had some other illness – she seemed to spend a large part of the day in bed. It was he who mainly looked after the child and they always finished on time so that he could take her to her nursery school. And how did he work? He dictated to her in the mornings, as I did, every so often sinking into silences that seemed to last for ever. He was always on his feet, pacing like a caged animal; one moment he was at the other end of the room, the next moment he was behind her. And he drank coffee – she'd already told me this. By the end of the day they'd only done about half a page. He rewrote it, changing every word, again and again, making her read the same sentence over and over. What was he writing? A new novel? What was it about? A novel, yes, about a sect of religious assassins. Or so it seemed for now, at least. She had lent him an annotated Bible of her father's, so he could check a quotation. And what did he think of himself? What did I mean? she asked. Did he consider himself *superior*? She thought for a moment, as if trying to remember something specific, some remark, something slipped into the conversation. 'He's never talked about his books,' she said doubtfully, 'but one day, as we were going over the same sentence for the tenth time, he said that a writer had to be a beetle and God at the same time.'

At the end of the first week, as I paid her, I noticed in the way she looked at the notes – the sudden focused attention, the satisfied care with which she put the money away – an intensity, a wave of interest, that made me see her for a moment in an unexpected light. Recalling her remark about how much Kloster paid her, I realised with surprise and slight alarm that money really did matter to the lovely Luciana.

What happened next? Well, a few things. There was a series of very hot days, an unexpected return of summer in mid-March, and Luciana swapped her blouses for short vests that exposed her shoulders as well as expanses of stomach and back. When she leaned forward to read from the screen I could see the gentle arch of her spine, and below the hollow of her back a spiral of blond downy hair extended to – and I could see it perfectly – the tiny and always troubling triangle of her panties peeping from her jeans. Was it deliberate? Of course not. It was all entirely innocent and we still looked at each other with the same innocent eyes, carefully avoiding touching in my narrow kitchen. It was in any case a new and very pleasant sight.

On one of these identically hot days, as I leaned over to check a sentence on the screen, I rested my hand, again innocently, on the back of the chair. She had shifted forward but now sat back, her shoulder against my hand, gently trapping it. Neither of us moved to break contact – that furtive but lengthy first contact – and, until we took our first break, I continued dictating standing, caught there touching her, feeling through my fingers, like an intense intermittent signal, a secret warm current, the heat of her skin from her neck to her shoulders.

A couple of days later I started dictating the first truly erotic scene of the novel. When I'd finished I asked her to read it back to me. I replaced a few words with cruder alternatives, and asked her to read it again. She complied, as unselfconscious as ever, and I could detect no agitation in her voice as she read the steamy passages. Even so, there was now a slight sexual tension in the air. I hoped, I said for the sake of saying something, that Kloster didn't subject her to such writing. She looked at me calmly and a little sardonically: she was used to it, she said, Kloster dictated things that were much worse. By a curious inflection of her voice, 'worse' seemed to mean *better*. A half-smile lingered on her lips, as if she were remembering something in particular, and I took it as a challenge. I went on dictating, waiting patiently for her to bend her neck from side to side. When at last I heard the bones crack I slid my hand under her hair and pressed the joint with my fingers. I think this irrevocable move – from avoiding touching her at all costs to touching her decisively – startled her as much as it did me, even as I tried to make it seem casual. She didn't move, didn't breathe, her hands away from the keyboard. She was staring straight ahead, and I couldn't decide whether she was hoping for something more or something less.

'When I get rid of this cast I'll give you a massage,' I said and moved my hand to the back of the chair.

'When you get rid of the cast you won't need me any more,' she answered, still not turning, smiling nervously, equivocally, as if she could see an opportunity to escape but hadn't yet decided if she wanted to take it.

'I could always break something else,' I said, and looked into her eyes. She looked away immediately.

'That would be no good: you know Kloster's getting back next week,' she said neutrally, as if she wanted, gently, to make me stop. Or was she simply testing me?

'Kloster, Kloster,' I said plaintively. 'Why should Kloster have *everything*?'

'I don't think he has everything he wants,' she said.

That was all she said, in the same even tone as before, but there was a quiet hint of pride in her voice. I thought I understood what she wanted me to understand. But if she was trying to cheer me up, she'd only added another source of irritation. So Kloster, who was so serious, had after all also had designs on our little Luciana. From what I'd just heard, he might even have already made a first move. And Luciana, far from slamming the door in his face, was about to go back to him. Kloster, now more enviable than ever even if he hadn't yet got very far with her, would have an opportunity every day. And as well as being proud that she was rejecting him, Luciana would also no doubt feel proud that he kept trying. Wasn't she at an age, just out of adolescence, when women want to test their powers of attraction on every man?

I imagined all of this from that slight inflexion of her voice, but couldn't make Luciana reveal anything more. As I started to probe, she said, blushing slightly, that she'd simply meant what she'd said: no one, not even Kloster, could have everything. That she wanted to deny it now simply served as confirmation and though I couldn't follow all its implications, I felt suddenly discouraged. There was an uncomfortable silence. Then she asked, almost imploringly, if we shouldn't continue working. Somewhat humiliated, I searched for the point in my manuscript where I'd stopped. I was mortified: I realised that in harping on Kloster so insistently I might have lost my chance. Had I ever had one? I'd thought I had with that first touch, despite her sudden stiffness. But now, as I continued dictating, it had all vanished, as if we'd both resumed our previous places, with a civilised distance between us. Nevertheless, as she picked up her bag before leaving, her eyes sought mine, as if she wanted to make sure of something, or, like me, she wanted to recover some of the contact that had been lost. This glance only disconcerted me all over again: it might mean simply that she didn't bear me a grudge but would rather forget what had just happened, or that the door, in spite of everything, was still open.

I waited impatiently for the day to end. The month had passed too quickly and I realised that there were only a couple of days left before Luciana disappeared from my life. When I let her in the next morning I looked to see if anything in her face or general appearance had changed since the day before – whether she'd tried a little more make-up, or a bit less clothing – but if anything she seemed to have succeeded in looking the same as always. And yet, nothing was the same. We sat down and I began dictating the last chapter of my novel. I wondered whether the imminent end wouldn't stir something in her as well, but as if we were applying ourselves with the utmost concentration to playing our parts, Luciana's hands, her head, her entire attention, seemed fully focused on my voice.

As the morning progressed, I realised I was waiting for a single movement. Strange dissociation. Though I still noticed the same things as usual – the gap between her T-shirt and the line of her panties, the seductively furrowed brow, the tips of her teeth biting her lip now and then, the movement of her shoulders as she leaned forward – it was strangely distant and all that I could really see before me, with extraordinary clarity, was the nape of her neck. I was waiting, with the pathetic expectancy of Pavlov's dog, for the moment when she would bend her neck from side to side. But the signal never came, as if she too had become conscious of the power, the danger, of that cracking sound. I waited incredulously, and then almost feeling as if I'd been cheated, till the very last moment, but her neck, her lovely capricious neck, remained stubbornly still, and I had to let that day go.

The next morning was our last. When Luciana arrived and dropped her tiny bag down beside her, it seemed simply inconceivable that I might no longer have her with me and that all these little routines would disappear. The first two hours passed, exasperatingly. During a break Luciana went to the kitchen to make coffee. This too was happening for the last time. I followed her and remarked, half humorous, half dejected, that next week she would be back to taking dictation of good novels. I told her of Campari's injunction when giving me her number, that I had to return her intact, and I added that to my regret I was complying. All this managed to draw from her was an uncomfortable smile. We went back to work. I only had a few pages of the epilogue left to dictate. I thought bitterly that we might even finish a little early that day. On one of the final pages there was a German street name and Luciana wanted me to check she'd spelled it correctly. I leaned over her shoulder to look at the screen, as I had done so many times in the past month, and once again I was enveloped in the scent of her hair. Then, just as I was about to move my hand from the back of the chair, like a belated call that I'd ceased to expect, she tilted her head to one side, almost touching me, then the other. I heard the crack and, as if it were a continuation of that first time, slid my hand beneath her hair until I found the gap between the vertebrae. She gave a small faltering sigh and leaned her head back, yielding to my touch. She turned her face towards me, expectantly. I kissed her once. She closed her eyes, and half opened them again. I kissed her more deeply and slid my left hand under her T-shirt. But the cast on my other hand hampered me and she was able to push the chair back slightly and free herself easily.

'What's the matter?' I asked, taken aback. I held out my hand, but something in her seemed to shrink from me and I froze.

'What's the matter?' She smiled nervously as she rearranged her hair. 'I've got a boyfriend, that's what's the matter.'

'But you had him ten seconds ago too,' I said, bewildered.

'Ten seconds ago . . . I forgot myself for a moment.'

'And now?'

'I remembered.'

'So what was it? A bout of amnesia?'

'I don't know,' she said, and she looked up, as if trying to make the whole thing seem trivial. 'You seemed to want it so much.'

'Ah,' I said, offended. 'Only *I* wanted it.'

'No,' she said, looking confused. 'I felt . . . curious. And you seemed so jealous of Kloster.'

'What's Kloster got to do with it?' I asked, exasperated. Competing against two other men seemed a bit much.

19

She seemed sorry she'd said it. She looked at me alarmed, I suppose because it was the first time she'd heard me raise my voice. 'No, no, nothing,' she said, as if she could take it back. 'I think I just wanted something to happen so you'd remember me.'

So she'd already learned that sort of trick, I thought bitterly. She was staring at me sadly, eyes open very wide, and she seemed to be both lying and telling the truth.

'Don't worry, I'll remember you,' I said, humiliated, but hoping to salvage some of my wounded pride. 'That's the first time anyone's kissed me out of pity.'

'Could we finish, please?' she said and cautiously edged the chair back in, as if fearing some kind of reprisal.

'Yes, of course, let's finish,' I said.

I dictated the last two pages. As she picked up her bag before leaving I handed her that week's pay without a word. For the first time she put it away without looking at it, as if she wanted to get away as quickly as possible.

That was the last time I saw Luciana, ten years ago, when she was just another very pretty girl, confident, carefree, trying her first games of seduction, far from matters of life and death.

The entry phone rang – it was five to four. As I went down in the lift, I stared at my now gaunt face in the mirror and couldn't help wondering what I would see when I opened the door.

2

Nothing could have prepared me for the sight of her. It was her, still Luciana, I had to admit it, but for a moment I thought there must be some terrible mistake. The terrible mistake of time. The cruellest revenge upon a woman, Kloster wrote, was to let ten years pass before seeing her again.

I could say that she'd put on weight, but that was the least of it. Perhaps the most appalling thing was the way the face I had once known tried to surface in her eyes, as if seeking me from a distant past, sunk in the black well of the years. She smiled with something like desperation, testing to see if she could count on even a part of the attraction she had once exerted over me. But the equivocal smile lasted only a fraction of a second, as if she knew that in a sequence of cruel amputations she had lost all her charms. My worst predictions for her appearance had come true. Her neck, the smooth neck that had come to obsess me, had thickened, and there was now an unmistakable roll of fat beneath her chin. The eyes that used to sparkle now looked small and puffy. Her mouth was drawn down at the corners in an embittered line, and it looked as if nothing had made her smile in a long time. But the worst thing was what had happened to her hair. An entire section had disappeared from the front, as if she'd suffered from some nervous disease, or she'd torn it out in fits of despair, and over the ear, where it was more sparse than elsewhere, whitish patches of scalp showed through, like terrible scars. My horrified, disbelieving stare must have lingered a little too long on the lank strands because she raised her hand to her ear to hide them, but gave up halfway, as if she knew the damage could not be concealed.

'Something else I owe Kloster,' she said.

She sat down in the same old swivel chair and looked around, surprised, I think, that the place had changed so little.

'Amazing,' she said, as if she found it unfair but was also relieved to have discovered a refuge, a piece of the past unexpectedly intact. 'Nothing's changed here. You've even kept that horrible little grey rug. And you . . .' She looked at me almost accusingly. 'You look just the same too. A few grey hairs maybe. You haven't even put on weight. I bet if I go to the kitchen the cupboards will be empty and all I'll find is coffee.'

It was my turn to say something pleasant, I suppose, but, unable to find the words, I let the moment pass and I think my silence pained her more than any lie.

'So,' she said with an ironic, disagreeable smile, 'don't you want to know how I am? Why don't you ask me about my boyfriend?' She said it as if this were some kind of guessing game.

'How's your boyfriend?' I asked mechanically.

'He's dead,' she said, but before I could say anything she fixed her gaze on mine, holding it steadily, as if it were still her turn. 'Why don't you ask me about my parents?' I said nothing and she answered her own question with the same defiant tone: 'They're dead. Why don't you ask me about my brother? He's dead.' Her lower lip trembled. 'Dead, dead, dead. One after the other. *And nobody realises*. At first even I didn't realise.'

'Do you mean someone killed them?'

'*Kloster*,' she said in a terrified whisper, leaning towards me as if someone might hear. 'And he hasn't finished yet. He does it slowly, that's the secret. He lets years go by.'

'Kloster is killing all your relatives, without anyone realising,' I said cautiously, as if humouring a mad person.

She nodded seriously, looking into my eyes, waiting for my reaction, as if she'd said the most important part and had put herself in my hands. Naturally I thought she must be suffering from some kind of mental disorder as a result of all these unfortunate deaths. Over the past few years Kloster had become almost obscenely famous: you couldn't open the papers without seeing his name. No other writer was as sought after, as ubiquitous, as celebrated. Kloster was a fixture on literary prize panels, heading the list of signatures to open letters, a delegate at international conferences and guest of honour at embassy receptions. Over the past ten years he had been transformed from well-kept secret to public property, almost a brand. His books were sold in all formats, from pocket editions to luxurious hardback volumes for the corporate gift market. And though he now had a frequently photographed face, I had long since ceased to think of him as a man, a person of flesh and bone: he'd vanished, become a name haunting bookshops, posters, headlines. Kloster now lived the hectic, unreachable life of a celebrity: he didn't seem to rest between book tours and all his other activities. Not to mention the hours he must have spent writing, because his novels continued to appear with calm regularity. The thought that Kloster might have something to do with real-life crimes was as outrageous as if she'd blamed the Pope.

'But Kloster?' I exclaimed involuntarily, unable to

shake off my astonishment. 'Surely he doesn't have time to plan murders?'

Too late I realised this could have sounded sarcastic and offended her. But Luciana replied as if I'd just provided her with the evidence that proved her theory conclusively.

'Precisely. That's part of his strategy – that nobody should think it possible. When I worked for you, you used to say he was a secret writer. In those days he despised anything to do with publicity. I heard him refuse interviews a hundred times. But in the past few years he's deliberately sought fame, because he needs it now: it's a perfect smokescreen. Or rather he *would* need it, if anyone bothered to look into it,' she said bitterly. 'If anyone was prepared to believe me.'

'But what motive could Kloster have for—'

'*I don't know.* That's the most exasperating part. Actually, he does have a motive: I sued him when I went back to work for him. But in hindsight it was a minor thing – it didn't even go to court. I can't believe he's still taking revenge: it's out of all proportion. The more I think about it the less I can believe it's the real reason.'

'You sued Kloster? But I thought he was the perfect boss. The last time I saw you, you seemed happy to be going back to work for him. What happened?'

The coffee pot on the hob started to hiss. I went to the kitchen, and returned with two cups of coffee. I waited for her to help herself to sugar. She stirred her coffee endlessly, as if she were trying to order her thoughts. Or maybe she was wondering how much to tell me.

'What happened? I've spent years asking myself every day what happened exactly. It's been a nightmare. I could recount each thing separately and it would just seem like a string of misfortunes. It all began when I went back to work for him, when he got back from his retreat. The first day he was in a good mood. During a break, while I was making coffee, he asked what I'd done during the month he was away. I told him, without a second thought, that I'd worked for you. At first he seemed simply intrigued. He asked who you were, and what the novel you were writing was about. I think he knew a little about you, or he pretended to. I told him you'd broken your wrist. It was just a casual conversation but there was something in his voice and his insistent questions that made me think he was jealous – he seemed to assume something had happened between you and me. A couple of times I think he was on the point of asking. And in the days that followed, every so often he'd somehow bring up my free month. He even read one of your books and made fun of it. I'd say nothing but that seemed to annoy him even more. A week later he changed tack. He became unusually silent. He hardly spoke to me and I thought he was going to fire me.'

'So I was right,' I said. 'He was in love with you.'

'Those days were the most difficult. He didn't dictate anything at all, just paced the room, as if he were trying to come to a decision that had nothing to do with his novel. Something about me. And suddenly, one morning, he started dictating again normally, as if nothing had happened. Actually, not quite normally: he seemed to be inspired. Until then he'd dictated at the most one or two paragraphs a day, going over them obsessively, line by line. But that day he dictated a long and rather horrifying scene in one go: a series of murders, throat-slittings by the religious assassins. He seemed transformed. He'd never dictated so fast – I had trouble keeping up. But I thought everything was OK again. I really needed that job so I was terribly worried about him firing me. He continued dictating at that pace for almost two hours and as we went on his mood seemed to get better and better. When I stopped to go and get more coffee, he even made a couple of jokes. I stood up and suddenly realised how stiff my neck was. I had a problem with it in those days,' she said, as if she were trying to prove her innocence with this belated explanation.

'Yes, I remember very well,' I said drily. 'Though I was always a bit suspicious of those neck aches of yours.'

'But I really did have a bad neck,' she said. It seemed vital to her that I believe it. There was a silence. She looked out of the window, lost in thought, as if she could still picture the scene, frozen in time. 'I had my back to him. I clicked my neck and suddenly felt him put his arm round me. I turned round and he . . . he tried to kiss me. I struggled to free myself but he was holding me firmly and didn't seem to notice, as if he just couldn't understand that I was resisting. So I screamed. Not too loudly: I just wanted him to let go. Actually I was more surprised than shocked. As I told you when you asked: I thought of him as a father. He froze. I think it was only then that he realised what he'd done and what could happen. His wife was upstairs and might have heard.

'There was a knock on the door and he went to open it. He was very pale. It was Pauli, his little girl. She'd heard me scream and asked, looking at me, what had happened. He told her not to worry – I'd seen a cockroach – and to go back to her room and play. We were alone again. As I gathered up my things, I said I'd never set foot in his house again. I was beside myself. I couldn't help crying and that made me even more furious. He asked if we could just forget the whole thing. He said it had all been a terrible mistake, but that it really hadn't been all his fault because I'd been *sending out signals*. And he said something even more insulting: he assumed I'd slept with you. I was incensed. I realised then, with absolute clarity, what had been going through his head. Before his trip he was crazy about me. He'd let me know in that unspoken way men have, but I don't think it had occurred to him to touch me. Since he'd got back, though, he'd thought of me as no more than a slut, with whom he too could try his luck. I screamed again and this time I didn't care if his wife heard. He moved closer as if to make me shut up and I said if he touched me again I'd sue him. He apologised and tried to calm me down. He opened the door and offered to pay me for the days I'd worked so far that month. I just wanted to get out of there as soon as I could. Outside I burst into tears again. It was my first job and I'd trusted him completely. I was home early and my mother saw immediately that I'd been crying. I had to tell her what had happened.'

She raised the cup of coffee with a trembling hand and took a sip. She appeared lost in the memory for a moment, staring into the cup.

'And what was her reaction?' I asked.

'She asked if I'd done anything to lead him on. She'd just been fired herself – that's why I went to work for Kloster – and now we'd both lost our jobs. She'd won some compensation so she thought we should go and see her solicitor. We agreed not to say anything to my father until it was all over. We went to see the solicitor that day. She was a terrifying woman – she scared *me*. Huge and fat, with tiny eyes, sitting bulging behind her desk. She looked like a union thug. She hated men, she told us; she was on a personal crusade against them and nothing pleased her more than crushing them. She called me "dear". She asked me to tell her the whole story. She said it was a pity he hadn't been a bit more insistent and that it had only happened that one time. She asked if I had any marks or bruises from the struggle. I had to tell her that there hadn't really been any physical violence. She said we wouldn't be able to sue him for sexual harassment but that she'd work something out, and slip the words in at the beginning just to make him nervous. The case, she explained, would ultimately be a claim for the social security and pension contributions he hadn't paid me. What had happened between us had taken place in a closed room, with no witnesses. It would be his word against mine so we wouldn't get far down that path. She asked if he was married and when I said yes she was delighted. She said the married ones were the easiest to scare: we could just name a figure and we'd get it out of him. On her calculator she added up the amount he'd have to pay me by law and then added an amount for compensation. It seemed like a fabulous sum, more than I'd ever earned in a whole year. She dictated the text of a letter for me to write. I asked if we couldn't change the accusation of sexual harassment in the heading to something less serious. She said that from now on I should get used to the idea that he was my enemy, and that he'd deny everything anyway.

'I went to the post office alone. I stood in the queue and felt a foreboding that I was about to set in motion something that would have irreparable consequences, that the letter had a hidden destructive power. I'd never felt like this before, as if I was about to fire a gun. I knew that one way or another I'd be doing him *harm*, and not just financially. I nearly turned round and came home. I think if I'd waited a day I'd never have sent the letter. But I'd come that far and I still felt humiliated. It seemed unfair that I'd lost my job, when I'd always behaved impeccably with him. In a way it seemed right that he should pay.'

'So you posted the letter.'

'Yes.'

She stared blankly into space again. After the first sip of coffee she'd put the cup down. She asked if she could smoke. I brought an ashtray from the kitchen and waited for her to go on, but the cigarette only seemed to take her further inside herself, to an obscure corner of her memory.

'You sent the letter . . . then what happened?'

'He didn't answer that first letter. I received a receipt: he'd got the letter, he'd read it, but he hadn't replied. After almost a month my mother phoned the solicitor. "Much better for us," the woman said. "Either he hasn't taken us seriously, or he's been very poorly advised." Again, I had a sense of foreboding. I'd worked for him for almost a year. You asked me once what he was like. At the time I thought he was the most intelligent man I had ever met – would ever meet. But there was also something just below the surface, something sinister, implacable – he was the last person I'd want to have as an enemy. I feared he'd take my letter as a declaration of war and that I'd have to face the worst of him. I was frightened and started having thoughts that were ... paranoid. After all, he had my address, my phone number. We'd become quite friendly; he knew a lot about me. I thought maybe he hadn't answered the letter because he was planning another kind of response, his own personal revenge. But the solicitor assured me that, as he was married, if he really was an intelligent man he'd do the only thing he could do: pay up. And the longer he took to reply, the higher the sum would get. She dictated a second letter, identical to the first, but demanding an even higher amount, because we were also claiming the wages for the month without a reply. It seemed to have an immediate effect. We received his first response, obviously also written by a solicitor. He rejected everything. It was a list of denials. He denied that I'd ever worked for him and even that he knew me. The solicitor told me not to worry. It was a stock legal reply and simply meant Kloster had realised we were serious and had got himself a lawyer. We now had to wait for the first conciliation meeting and think about how much lower a sum we would accept. I was reassured. In the end it all seemed impersonal, an administrative formality.'

'So you went to the conciliation meeting.'

Luciana nodded. 'I asked my mother to come with me because I was scared of facing Kloster again. Ten minutes after the agreed time there was still no sign of him. The solicitor whispered, as if it was just a little bit of mischief, that he was probably busy with another bigger case: his divorce. She said a colleague who was a friend of hers was acting for Kloster's wife. Apparently his wife had read my letter, with the accusation of sexual harassment, and decided to file for divorce immediately. She'd asked for a settlement running into millions. And her friend was ruthless, the solicitor said: Kloster would be out on the street. I listened, horrified. It had never even occurred to me this might happen.

'Another five minutes passed and at last Kloster's solicitor appeared. He seemed like a calm, courteous man. He said he had instructions to offer us two months' pay as compensation. My solicitor rejected this outright, without even consulting me, and the second conciliation meeting was set for a month later. This would give everyone, the mediator said, time to reflect and come closer to an agreement. Outside I asked my mother if we shouldn't just drop the whole thing. I'd never wanted things to go that far; I never imagined I'd end up destroying his marriage. My mother got annoyed with me: she didn't understand how I could feel sorry for him. His marriage must have been long over for him to try something with me. So I didn't say any more. Actually, I felt afraid, rather than sorry. My worst fears were being realised. After all, he'd only tried to kiss me. The consequences seemed excessive, out of control.

'As the days passed I grew more and more anxious. I just wanted to get to the next meeting and for it all to end. I was prepared to stand up to my mother and my own solicitor so that we accepted whatever the other side offered. A day before the date set the mediator telephoned: the meeting was being postponed for a week. I was put out, and asked why. She said it was at the request of the other party. I asked if they were allowed to change the date just like that. She said yes, in extreme circumstances, and lowered her voice: *Kloster's little girl had died*. I couldn't believe it, but at the same time, strangely, I did believe it and accepted it, in all its awfulness, as if it were the logical, ultimate consequence of what my letter had started. I don't think I said anything for a moment but eventually I managed to ask what had happened. The mediator only knew what Kloster's solicitor had told her: apparently it was a domestic accident.

'After I hung up I went to my desk, to find the drawings Pauli had given me. She'd drawn her daddy looking huge and me on a tiny chair. The computer was a little square, and at the bottom she'd written her name, which she'd just learned to do. In the second picture, there was an open door, with the daddy in the distance, looking tiny, and she and I were holding hands, almost the same height, as if we were sisters. They were happy, carefree pictures. And now she was dead. I cried all afternoon. I think I was crying for myself too. Although I didn't yet know when or how, I sensed that it wouldn't stop there and that something terrible was going to happen to me.'

'But why did you think that? If it was an accident, why would he hold you responsible?'

'I don't know. I don't know exactly why. But that was what I felt right from the start and, most of all, I think it was what he felt too. It's the only explanation I can find for everything that happened afterwards.'

She paused and lit another cigarette with trembling hands.

'So you went to the second conciliation meeting,' I said.

She nodded. 'Like before, my mother and I arrived first and we were shown into the mediation room. We waited a few minutes with our solicitor. I thought Kloster would send his lawyer again. But when the door opened it was Kloster who entered. He was alone. His face was shockingly changed, as if he had died with his daughter. He'd lost a huge amount of weight and looked as if he hadn't slept in days. His eyes were red and his cheeks sunken. He was incredibly pale, as if all the blood had been drawn from his body. But even so, he looked composed and resolute, as if he had a task to accomplish and no time to lose. He was carrying a book that I recognised immediately: it was my father's annotated Bible which I'd lent him. He crossed the room, straight towards me. My mother made a move as if to protect me. I don't think he even noticed. He was only looking at me, with a terrible stare that I still see every night. He blamed me, without a doubt. He stopped and held out the Bible without a word. I put it quickly in my bag. He turned to the mediator and asked how much we were claiming in compensation. He listened to the figure and took a chequebook from his pocket, opening it out on the desk. The mediator started to say that he could of course make a counter-offer, but he held up his hand to stop her, as if he didn't want to hear another word about the matter. He wrote out three cheques: one to me for the total amount we'd claimed, and another two for the mediator's and my lawyer's fees. I signed a document stating that the claim was settled. He picked up his copy, turned round without looking at anyone and left. The whole thing took under ten minutes. The mediator could hardly believe it; it was the first time a case had ever ended like this.'

'Then what happened?'

'Then . . . I went home, took the Bible from my bag and put it on the shelf above my desk, with my university course books. It was a Bible my father no longer used and it was months since I'd lent it to Kloster: I'd forgotten all about it. In fact, when I thought about the meeting again, it occurred to me that it had been an excuse to come up close and stare at me in that way. I couldn't get that out of my head and I had nightmares for days afterwards. I dreamed that Kloster's little girl was taking my hand, wanting me to come and play with her, and saying, just as she had when she was alive, that she didn't want to be on her own in the room next door any more.

'I opened a bank account and paid in the cheque, but the days passed and I couldn't bring myself to touch the money. For a time I thought of donating it to charity, but I had a superstitious fear of doing anything with it, even to give it away, as if like that I'd be able to keep things from moving on. I thought that as soon as I withdrew even a tiny amount it would trigger reprisals. I became obsessed with the idea that Kloster was planning something terrible against me and that was why he'd agreed to pay the money without argument. I told my boyfriend some of this but I never mentioned that Kloster had tried to kiss me. All I said was that I'd brought a claim for unfair dismissal against him, that he'd lost a lot of money, and I was afraid he was going to take revenge somehow. At that time Kloster had a novel published. Not the one he'd been dictating to me but another one that he'd completed before I started working for him. The one he'd edited on his retreat in Italy.'

'*The Day of the Dead*. I remember it well. It came out at the same time as the one I dictated to you. It was his first big hit.'

'It soon became a bestseller. It topped all the lists, was in all the shop windows. You could even find it in supermarkets. Every time I passed a bookshop I'd see his name and shiver. My boyfriend tried to reassure me, saying it must have earned Kloster much more than what he'd paid me and he had probably forgotten all about it. But I started noticing something.'

'What?'

'What we mentioned before. Until then, as you said, Kloster was a writer who hated public appearances. But suddenly he became *famous*. As if he wanted to be everywhere, all the time.'

'Maybe it was because he was alone – it was a way of filling time.'

'Yes, at first I thought something like that as well, that he was looking for comfort in celebrity, or trying to keep his mind busy so as to forget his daughter's death. Even so, it went totally against his nature. It made me suspect it was part of his plan. But my boyfriend convinced me that Kloster was too busy promoting his book to think of me. That year Ramiro had finished his course in physical education and found a job as a lifeguard on one of the beaches in Villa Gesell. But he wanted to spend time in Mexico before starting. He'd been planning the trip for some time and asked me to go with him, to forget all about the Kloster business. It seemed like a good idea and I used part of the compensation money for it. We spent almost a month longer than we'd intended travelling around, visiting little Mexican villages, and we got back at the beginning of December, in time for him to start work. I stayed in Buenos Aires to sit my finals, but my parents and Valentina and Bruno were already in Gesell so as soon as I finished my exams I took the overnight bus there. I wanted to surprise Ramiro and went straight from the bus station to the beach, so we could have breakfast together. We sat at a little bar on the beach. It was early, and there weren't many people about. I looked around and saw a man in swimming trunks and goggles at a neighbouring table. He was tanned, as if he'd already been there a few days. I almost cried out when I recognised him: it was Kloster. He was having a coffee and reading the paper, pretending not to see me, though he was only a few feet away.'

'Couldn't it simply have been a coincidence? Lots of writers used to spend the summer in Gesell. Maybe he was renting a house there.'

'Of all the resorts on the coast he chose Gesell? Of all the bars, he went to the very one near my boyfriend's job? No. It was odd enough that he'd picked Gesell. He knew I spent every summer there. I pointed him out discreetly to Ramiro and he said it could be a coincidence as well. I asked if it was the first time he'd seen him. He said he'd been there every morning, sitting at the same table, for about a week. After reading the paper he'd wade into the sea and swim out very far. Actually I think Ramiro was a bit surprised, and a bit jealous, that this was the writer I'd worked for. I'd told him very little about Kloster and I suppose he'd pictured him much older, more bookish. Sitting there in his trunks Kloster looked like an athlete. He'd regained some of the weight he'd lost, and the sun and sea air had obviously done him good.

'While Ramiro and I were talking about him, he went to the water's edge and swam out with long, relaxed strokes until he was beyond the breaker. He went further and further out. At first you could still see his arms rising out of the water, but once he got beyond the last line of buoys he was just a dot that became harder and harder to make out in the waves. At one stage I lost sight of him completely. Ramiro passed me his binoculars. I could see him still swimming with the same placid strokes, as if he'd only just set off. I asked Ramiro what would happen if he suddenly got cramp so far out. He admitted that most probably he wouldn't get there in time to save him. So how could he let him swim out so far? I asked. He seemed embarrassed and said that it was a sort of code: Kloster was a grown-up and obviously knew what he was doing.

'I looked through the binoculars again and said I was amazed he could still be swimming at the same pace. I regretted saying it immediately. Ramiro seemed piqued and said that he swam out just as far every morning, as part of his training for the job. We said nothing more until Kloster reappeared, swimming on his back. He turned round at the last moment, before being dragged in by the breakers, shook his streaming hair from his face, and strode out of the water. He didn't look in the least bit tired. Still dripping with water, he walked right past without glancing at us, picked up his things from the table, settled the bill, and left. I asked Ramiro if he ever came back in the afternoon and he said no. Nor had he ever seen him in town in the evening.

'We had a bit of an argument then. I begged him not to have breakfast there any more and to go to the bar next door. He was annoyed and asked why he should. I couldn't tell him the true reason. I wasn't really sure myself what I was afraid of. I said I wanted to have breakfast there with him every morning but it made me uncomfortable having Kloster so near. He said he couldn't leave his post, and didn't see why he should have to move. Kloster should be the one to find himself another bar. His anger made me feel there was something he wasn't telling me.'

She stopped suddenly and leaned forward to stub out her cigarette, twisting and turning it in the ashtray, as if there were one particular memory she found humiliating that made it difficult to go on. She lit another cigarette and as she expelled the first cloud she waved her hand, but I couldn't tell whether it was simply to disperse the smoke or in unconscious recognition that none of it mattered now. She took another drag on her cigarette and seemed to find the strength to continue.

'In fact I don't think he liked me having breakfast with him. There was a waitress there who was really pretty and sexy. She always wore tiny miniskirts and bikini tops. As soon as I saw her I thought there were too many giggles and glances between them. When I said this, he got even angrier and denied it, of course. But I really believed he was in danger and I wasn't prepared to go away and leave him alone just because of a jealous scene. So I went back the following morning. I got there a little earlier. Kloster arrived soon afterwards, before we'd ordered. But instead of sitting at one of the tables outside, he went in and sat at the bar. At first I took this as a good sign, an admission that he'd seen me but didn't want to face me. I wondered for a moment if perhaps, as Ramiro had said, it really was a coincidence that Kloster was there. I didn't want to look in his direction and when the waitress had brought our coffee I tried to chat to Ramiro as if Kloster didn't exist – and the waitress as well. I think Ramiro was even more pleased than I was that Kloster had gone inside and things could stay as they were. He was in a good mood and as soon as he finished breakfast he ran down to the sea, leapt over the breakers and swam out. I suppose he wanted to impress me. I watched as he grew more and more distant, beyond the buoys. He'd left the binoculars on the table and I followed him for a while. His strokes were more energetic than Kloster's and he was splashing a lot as he kicked his feet, but he didn't seem to be gliding through the water as smoothly as Kloster had. And he looked as if he was getting tired: he was twisting awkwardly when he lifted his head from the water to take a breath, he was losing his rhythm and his strokes were becoming jerky. He stopped and floated on his back for a while, resting. I thought he seemed agitated . . . exhausted. I don't think he was half as far out as Kloster had been the day before. Even without the binoculars I could still make out his head and shoulders in the water. He swam back more slowly and when he was close to the shore, to show off or something, he did the butterfly for the last few yards. I think it was intended for the waitress rather than me. When he got out, breathing hard, I suddenly realised what Kloster's plan was.'

'Swim out really far and pretend to get cramp, making the lifeguard swim out further than he can manage and become exhausted. Drown the lifeguard.'

'Yes, something like that. I assumed he was waiting for a day when the sea was rough. Then when Ramiro had exhausted himself, swimming out, Kloster would duck him under and drown him. If they were far out enough, at that time of day no one would see.'

'Perhaps only you, with the binoculars.'

43

'That's what I found most chilling: he wanted to kill Ramiro in front of me. And afterwards it would be his word against mine. It seemed so incredible, so unreal, I couldn't tell anyone. At that very moment there were people nearby on sun loungers reading Kloster's latest novel. And while I was imagining all this Kloster was inside, at the bar, quietly having coffee and reading the paper, apparently not even aware of us. A little later he went for a swim, going out as far as the day before. Then he left, without even glancing in our direction.'

'And then?'

'Then ... There were two or three more mornings that went the same. Kloster would sit at the bar and read the paper. He only passed by us when he went for a swim. When he was in the sea I was trembling inside and I had to keep watching him until he came back and left. I realised that he was going out a little further each time. I think Ramiro had noticed too, and, as if it were some sort of competition – macho nonsense – he tried to swim just as far. Then we had the row about the cup of coffee.'

'The cup of coffee?'

'Yes. I asked again if we could switch to a different bar. Another one had opened, nearer his post. That left him no excuse. He got annoyed and asked why we should move when it didn't look as if Kloster had any intention of bothering us. Or had something else happened between him and me? I knew he was only pretending to be jealous – he just didn't want to have to stop ogling the waitress's tits. I said I was fed up with the little tart bringing me my coffee cold. It was true: she seemed to do it deliberately. He hadn't even noticed because he quite liked his coffee lukewarm. We started arguing and he told me not to bother having breakfast with him any more if I was just doing it to keep an eye on him. He said I could go and find another bar myself and leave him alone. I went home in tears. My mother and Valentina were about to go out mushroom gathering so I went with them. It was my parents' anniversary the next day and my mother always made a mushroom pie, which only she and my father liked. Actually, I don't think Daddy really did, but he'd never dared tell her because it was the first thing she'd ever cooked for him and she was very proud of her recipe. We always went to the same place to pick the mushrooms, a little wood behind the house where very few people ever went. My mother considered it to be almost an extension of our garden.

'When Valentina was out of earshot I told my mother about the row. She was surprised and a little alarmed to hear that Kloster was there. She asked why I hadn't told her about it immediately. She wanted to know if he'd tried to talk to me and I said that since he'd seen me he'd had his coffee inside the bar and had never come near me. This seemed to reassure her. I almost told her what I was really afraid of, but my mother thought I'd become a little obsessed with the death of Kloster's daughter. At the time she even suggested I see a therapist. I couldn't see how to tell her that I thought Kloster was planning a murder without its sounding crazy. I ended up telling her about the waitress and my row with Ramiro. She laughed and said I should go back the next day and have breakfast with him as if nothing had happened and it would all work out. My mother was terribly fond of Ramiro and she couldn't believe the quarrel was serious.'

'And you listened to her?'

'Yes, unfortunately, I did. When I arrived Ramiro had already got his food; he hadn't even waited for me. Kloster was already there, in his usual place, at the bar. It was a cool, blowy morning and the sea was rough. The water was murky, with a big swell and spray flying in the wind. I ordered coffee with milk and when the girl finally deigned to bring it to me it was, of course, cold, but I didn't say anything. Actually, neither of us said much. The silence was horribly tense. When Ramiro finished his coffee he took off his tracksuit to go for a swim. I asked if it wasn't dangerous with the sea so rough. He said he'd rather go in the water than stay there with me. And then he said something even more hurtful that still makes me cry when I think of it. I watched him dive into the first big breaker and emerge on the other side. He had to swim through quite a few big waves until he got beyond the end of the breakwater, where it was a bit calmer. But he still seemed to be having trouble. Because the sea was so rough I'd lose sight of him every so often, but he'd reappear, a tiny dot in the waves. At one stage I couldn't see him at all and when his head reappeared it looked as if he was waving to me desperately. I was frightened and I grabbed his binoculars, and when I spotted him again he was going under. I jumped up, terrified. The beach was empty and immediately I thought of Kloster. Not caring about anything, I ran inside the bar to beg him for help. But when I opened the door I saw that *Kloster was no longer there*. Can you believe it? He was the only one who could have saved him, but when I went into the bar he'd left. He'd left!'

'So what did you do?'

'I ran to the next breakwater to get the lifeguards, and the owner of the bar called the lifeboat. It took them almost an hour to retrieve the body. By the time the boat got back to shore a crowd had gathered, as if to witness the landing of a huge fish. Children were shouting with excitement and running to tell their parents: "A drowned man! A drowned man!" The lifeguards had laid a blanket over him but his hands were uncovered. They were blue, with a tracery of white veins. They carried him on a stretcher to the promenade where an ambulance was waiting. A woman police officer came over and asked me for his parents' phone number. It all seemed like a bad dream. My legs gave way. Then, as if from somewhere very far away, I heard people shouting at me and felt them patting my face. I opened my eyes for a moment and saw a crowd of strangers around me and the face of the policewoman peering at me. I wanted to grab her arm and scream, "Kloster! Kloster!" but I fainted again.

'When I came to I was in hospital. I'd been given a tranquilliser and had been out for twenty-four hours. My mother told me it was all over. A routine post-mortem had shown asphyxia by immersion, probably caused by hypothermia and cramp – the water that day had been very cold. Ramiro's parents had arrived from Buenos Aires and returned immediately with the body so as to hold the wake there. Then I told my mother about what had happened that morning, as I remembered it: my despair when I saw Ramiro go under and how I'd run to get Kloster and found that he wasn't in the bar. The only day he'd left early, without going for a swim. My mother didn't find this odd: it had been obvious that the sea was dangerous that morning. The hazard flag had been up on all the beaches since first light and prob-ably Kloster had decided, quite rightly, to go home and leave his swim for another day. When I insisted that I found it suspicious, my mother looked worried. "It was an accident," she said. "God's will." I think she was afraid I was going to start obsessing about Kloster again. She refused to discuss it any more, at least not till I was out of hospital.'

'You think Kloster saw that your boyfriend was drowning and went home, leaving him to die?'

'No. From where he was sitting he could hardly see the sea. It wasn't that. Or at least it wasn't just that. I didn't know exactly how but he'd achieved what he'd set out to do: to have Ramiro die before my eyes.'

'Did you go back to the beach during that time? Did you see Kloster again?'

'I did, but not immediately. I stayed in my room, crying. I couldn't stop thinking about the way Ramiro had looked annoyed and left to go for his swim. And the insulting thing he said. It was my last memory of him. I couldn't bring myself to go back to that beach for two or three days. I was truly afraid of Kloster now and felt too weak to confront him. Then I did go back very early one morning. There was a new lifeguard and, with the usual throng of people in January, everything seemed different. I looked inside the bar: Kloster wasn't there. I went in and talked for a while with the owner. She said that the writer, as they called him, had left the day after Ramiro drowned. He said he had to get back to Buenos Aires to start on a new novel. I sat at the bar, at the place where Kloster always sat, and looked out at the table on the beach where Ramiro and I used to sit for breakfast. I wanted to see through his eyes. You could just see those few tables and the lifeguard's chair. At low tide you couldn't even see the line of the breakers. I stayed there a long time, until another couple sat down at what had been our table and I felt like crying. I realised I didn't want to spend another day in Gesell so that evening I came back to Buenos Aires.'

'So was that all? You didn't speak to Ramiro's parents?'

'I did. I went to see them as soon as I got back. But I'd gone over and over it in my mind and had gradually accepted that it couldn't be anything other than a terrible accident. What could I have said to them? That out of a desire for revenge, for having been sued for a few thousand pesos, Kloster had somehow engineered Ramiro's death? I mean, I hadn't seen anything more than an accident, and when I spoke to them they were already resigned to it, and even a little embarrassed that Ramiro had been so reckless. His mother had always been very religious: she was a member of the same church as my father. She spoke of the peace that follows grief, when you finally accept someone's death. As I left their house I too experienced a strange sense of calm, for the first time in ages. I felt that whatever Kloster had wanted he'd undoubtedly achieved it, and that our respective tragedies had made us quits. That with Ramiro's death, however sinister it might seem, some sort of balance had been restored. One death each. I tried to forget the whole business and for a few months my life almost went back to normal. I think I would even have forgotten about

Kloster had it not been for the fact that his name was in the papers more and more often and his books seemed to be in all the shop windows.

'A year passed. December came and I felt I didn't want to spend the holidays in Gesell as usual. I thought the sea and the beach would bring back too many bad memories, so I stayed in Buenos Aires. The rest of the family left just after Christmas and I spent the time preparing for another exam. So I wouldn't forget, I put a note in my diary to phone my parents on their anniversary. I think I would have remembered anyway: it was the day before the date of Ramiro's death. I waited till the evening to phone. I assumed they'd spent the day at the beach and I wanted to be sure to find them at home.'

She fell silent, as if a hidden cog in her memory had come to a halt. She stared at the cup she'd placed to one side and, as she bowed her head, the tears fell silently, as if she'd only just held them back till then. When she looked up again, teardrops still clung to her lashes. Embarrassed, she wiped them away quickly with the back of her hand.

'I rang at ten. My mother answered the phone. She sounded happy, in a good mood. She'd made her mushroom pie, and she and my father had had dinner alone. My brother Bruno had gone out with his girlfriend and Valentina was staying the night at a friend's house. She said they missed me and that it wasn't the same without me. I said the wine had made her sentimental. She laughed and said yes, they had had some wine to celebrate. Then I spoke to my father for a minute or two. We joked about the mushroom pie. He said he'd eaten it all, like a good husband. He too sounded slightly emotional and he made me promise I'd go and see them one weekend. Before hanging up, he blessed me, the way he used to when we were small. I was very tired that night and fell asleep in front of the TV. I was woken at five by the telephone: it was Bruno, my brother. He was calling from the hospital in Villa Gesell: my parents had been rushed there with violent stomach cramps. Initial tests showed traces of a fungus called *Amanita phalloides*. It's terribly poisonous but can easily be mistaken for edible species. Bruno had finished his medical studies by then so he had been able to have a frank talk with the doctors. He said we had to prepare for the worst: the toxins had spread through their digestive systems and could fatally damage their livers in a few hours. He'd requested they be transferred here to Buenos Aires, to the Hospital de Clinicas, where he was a junior doctor. He thought they might have a chance if they could get liver transplants. He said he'd go with them in the ambulance. I went to wait for him at the hospital. As soon as I saw his face, I knew they'd died on the way there.'

She fell silent again, as if her thoughts were once more far away.

'Could your mother have made a mistake when she picked the mushrooms?'

She shook her head hopelessly. 'That was what I found hardest to believe. She always went to the same spot to pick them and there had never been any poisonous species there. She had a mushroom guide and she'd shown us the pictures and taught us to recognise the different kinds, but never, in all the summers we spent there, did we see a single poisonous specimen. That's why she even let Valentina accompany her. There was an investigation immediately, which said that it was an accident, regrettable, but not unprecedented. Woods without toxic species can easily become contaminated from one season to the next. Each fungus has thousands of spores and a gust of wind is all that's needed to spread them quite a distance. And this species of *Amanita* is particularly difficult to distinguish from edible species, even for people who are quite experienced. The only visible difference is the volva, a white swollen sac at the base of the stem. But the mushroom can often come away from the base, or else the volva can be buried, or concealed by leaf litter. After my parents' death, some were actually found in the wood. They were almost hidden, and an inexperienced mushroomer could have been fooled. According to the report it had been silly to allow a child of Valentina's age to go mushroom picking. They thought that it was probably Valentina who gathered the poisonous fungi without noticing the volva and that my mother didn't recognise them once they'd been detached from the base.'

'But what was your hypothesis?'

'*Kloster*. It was him again. He'd reappeared, when I thought it was all over. I knew it as soon as I got Bruno's call. When he mentioned the name of the fungus, I felt that if I opened my mouth I would just start screaming. Because it was me who had given Kloster the idea.'

'You gave him the idea? What do you mean?'

'From time to time, during the year I worked for him, he had me cut out and keep police reports from the newspaper that interested him for one reason or another. Once he made me cut out an article about a grandmother who'd accidentally cooked poisonous fungi for herself and her granddaughter. They both died in agony a few hours later. What attracted his attention was that the grandmother considered herself an authority on wild mushrooms. He said that experts were often also the most careless, and when devising murders for his novels he was always interested in this – the mistakes made by such experts. In the article it mentioned in passing that the poisonous fungi were of that very same variety, *Amanita phalloides*. I explained to him why it was so easy to mistake them for edible mushrooms. I even drew him a picture, with the cap, the stem, the ring and the volva. I told him about other less well-known but dangerous types. I was proud to display my knowledge. He was surprised and asked me how I knew all this, so I told him . . . I told him everything: how my mother had taught all three of us, showing us the pictures from her book. The little wood behind the house at Villa Gesell. The mushroom pie on their wedding anniversary. The joke with my father about his sacrifice once a year.'

'But he didn't know the actual date of their anniversary, did he?'

'Yes. He knew, and I don't think he forgot it. The twenty-eighth of December. When I mentioned it to him he asked if my parents had chosen the date for any particular reason. He'd read in one of his books on religion that after the massacre of the Holy Innocents many Christian couples chose that date for their wedding day as a symbol of the will to overcome death, the beginning of a new cycle. And there was another thing: I hadn't seen him since Ramiro's death. But on the day of my parents' funeral, as we were leaving the cemetery, he was there.'

'You mean he went to your parents' funeral?' I asked doubtfully.

'No. I saw him in the distance, in a side avenue, by one of the graves – his daughter's, I suppose. He was kneeling, with his hand on the gravestone, and he seemed to be talking to it. At least, I could see his lips moving. But I think he went there deliberately that day, so that I'd see him.'

'Couldn't it have been a coincidence? Maybe it was

his daughter's birthday. Or the day of the week he always visited the grave.'

'No, her birthday was in August. I think he was only there for one reason: he wanted me to see him, so that I'd know that these deaths were part of his revenge as well. That we weren't quits, as I'd thought. In fact he warned me about it at the beginning. He spelled it out quite clearly. I just didn't understand.'

'What did he spell out?'

'What was going to happen to me. But you won't believe me if I tell you. My own brother didn't believe me. You have to see for yourself.' She leaned forward, as if she'd decided to reveal part of it. 'It has to do with the Bible he returned at the conciliation meeting.' Her voice grew quieter and quieter as she said this until she stopped, her eyes fixed on me, as if she'd told me her most jealously guarded secret and wasn't sure if I was worthy of the revelation.

'Have you brought it with you?' I asked.

'No, I couldn't bring myself to. I don't dare take it out of the house because it's my only proof against him. I wanted to ask you to come with me now, so that I can show it to you.'

'Now?' I said, unable to stop myself glancing at my watch. It was getting dark and I realised I'd been listening to her for over three hours. But Luciana didn't seem ready to release me.

'Yes, we could go now. It's only a short journey on the subway; it won't take long. Actually I was going to ask if you'd see me home anyway. Lately I've been terrified of going home alone after dark.'

Why did I say yes when everything inside me said no? Why didn't I fob her off with some excuse and put as much distance between us as I could? There are times in life – not many – when you can see, with dizzying clarity, the fatal fork in the road represented by one small act, the catastrophe that lurks behind a trivial decision. That evening I knew, above all else, that I shouldn't listen to her any more. But, overcome by the inertia of compassion, or politeness, I stood up and followed her out.

3

We walked in the cold to the subway. It was almost supper time and, with all the shops shut, the city looked dark and lifeless. People were heading home and the streets had the silent deserted quality of Sundays at dusk. Along the avenue, which was a little busier, I had to hurry to keep up with Luciana. Now, outdoors, all the signs of her nervousness became more pronounced, as if she really believed someone was pursuing her. Every three or four steps she turned her head compulsively and at street corners she looked to left and right, studying the people and the cars. When we stopped at traffic lights she chewed furtively at her fingers, and her eyes darted about incessantly. On the platform she stood well behind the yellow line, glancing over her shoulder at anyone who came near. During the journey, which was very short, we hardly exchanged a word, as if it required all her attention to scan the faces in the carriage and scrutinise the few passengers who got on at each stop. She seemed to calm down only once we had left the subway and turned a corner, when she pointed out her building, halfway down the block, as if it were a secure fortress reached after a perilous journey. Her apartment was on the top floor, she said, indicating a large balcony high above, jutting out over the street. We went up in the lift in silence and emerged on to a narrow landing with parquet flooring and doors, marked A and B, at either end. Luciana turned left and unlocked the door to her apartment with a slightly shaky hand. I followed her into a large L-shaped living room. She hurried to the window framing the black night and drew the curtains with a look of annoyance. She said she'd told her sister a thousand times to close the curtains before she went out – she hated getting back in the evening and seeing the blackness through the window. But her sister seemed to defy her deliberately.

'Where is she now?' I asked.

'At a friend's house. They run the school magazine together. They have to design the cover. She said she'd be back late, and might even stay the night there.'

She said this without looking at me, as she picked up a cup that had been left on the sideboard and lit a lamp on a glass side table. She switched off the central light and the room was plunged into shadow. I remained standing, reluctant to sit in the armchair she'd cleared of papers, with the growing feeling of having fallen into a trap. Luciana looked at me, as if suddenly noticing that I hadn't moved.

'I could make us something to eat, if you like.'

'No,' I said, and looked at my watch. 'Thanks. I'll just have a coffee. I can only stay half an hour. I've got to prepare my class for tomorrow.'

She fixed me now with her eyes, and I held her gaze as best I could. She seemed offended, even humiliated, as if she'd read my mind: at one time I'd have given anything for such an offer.

'You said it wouldn't take long,' I said, growing more and more uncomfortable. 'That's why I came back with you. But I've got to give a class first thing tomorrow.'

'That's fine,' she said. 'I'll get you some coffee. You can sit down, at least.'

She went to the kitchen and I sat in one of the solemn squashy armchairs arranged about the coffee table. I looked around: a chandelier, dark heavy furniture, a metal crucifix on one wall, a small bookcase full of knick-knacks. It felt like a place frozen in time, the severe old-fashioned décor no doubt chosen by the mother many years ago, the furniture perhaps inherited, and the daughters, now alone, lacking the strength to change it. A photograph in a silver frame stood beside the lamp.

There they all were, on a beach, probably in Villa Gesell, looking happy and suntanned: the father standing, holding a sunshade, the mother with a basket, and the three children sitting in the sand, as if they didn't want to leave. I could see Luciana, slim again and terribly young, behind her sister. Luciana as I had once known her. I almost had to close my eyes to dispel the image. I could hear her coming back from the kitchen so I hurriedly put the frame down, but didn't manage to unfold the stand in time. Luciana placed the tray on the table, then took the photograph and looked at it for a moment.

'It's the last photo of us all together,' she said. 'It was the summer before I met you. My brother Bruno hadn't graduated yet. And I was the same age Valentina is now. Only I think I was a little more mature than she is,' she added and put the photograph down. She took a sip of coffee and then stood up again, as if she'd forgotten the most important thing. 'I'll bring the Bible,' she said.

She disappeared down the hallway that led to the bedrooms and was away for two or three minutes. When she came back, once again I felt the alarm verging on fear that the madness of others inspires. She wore a pair of latex gloves and held the large book out in front of her, as if she were the high priestess in some private ritual bearing a fragile relic. Under her arm she gripped an oblong cardboard box. She put the book on the table and held out the box to me.

'I used this sort of gloves at university for experiments in the lab,' she said. 'Kloster's fingerprints are on the page and it's the only evidence I have against him. I don't want them to get smudged with other fingerprints.'

I put on a pair of the gloves, with difficulty because they were too small, and swore to myself that it was the last favour she would get out of me. Once I had donned the gloves she slid the book towards me. It was an impressive volume, rather beautiful, with a tooled leather cover, gilded edges to the pages and a red ribbon as a marker.

'The night my parents died, when Bruno phoned, I remembered the Bible Kloster had returned to me at the conciliation meeting. After I'd hung up, before leaving for the hospital, I opened it at the page where the bookmark was. Kloster handed it to me as it is now, with the marker at this page.'

I opened the Bible at the marked page, near the beginning. It was the part in the Old Testament about the first murder – Abel's death at the hands of his brother Cain – and Cain's final plea, when God condemns him to exile. I read aloud, doubtfully, as I wasn't sure it was the paragraph she meant: '"Behold, thou hast driven me out this day from the face of the earth; and from thy face shall I be hid; and I shall be a fugitive and a vagabond in the earth; and it shall come to pass, that every one that findeth me shall slay me."'

'A little further on: God's promise to Cain.'

'"And the Lord said unto him, Therefore whosoever slayeth Cain, vengeance shall be taken on him sevenfold."'

'*Vengeance shall be taken on him sevenfold.* Do you see? That was the line Kloster wanted me to read. The line intended for me. When I was working for him he dictated a novel that was never published, about a Cainite sect that took this notion of proportion literally in avenging their own. Divine law, as laid down for them by God, wasn't an eye for an eye, a tooth for a tooth. It was seven for one.'

She had again fixed her gaze on me anxiously, watching my face for the slightest hint of scepticism. I handed back the Bible and removed the gloves.

'Seven for one. But it hasn't been carried out exactly, has it?' I said. I realised I was beginning to feel truly afraid of her.

'My God, can't you see? It's taking place step by step. And if no one realises what's happening, if no one stops him, he'll just keep going.'

'But I still don't understand,' I said, 'how it could have been him in the first two cases you've told me about.'

'Yes, that was what was driving me most crazy. From the moment I opened the Bible and read that sentence I no longer had any doubt that it was him, but I still couldn't see how he'd done it on either occasion. It was all I could think about. I even stopped eating during that time. I was in a kind of fever that prevented me from doing anything else. Actually I had an idea how he'd done it in my parents' case. All he had to have done was follow me to the house that first summer and he'd have seen the little wood where we picked mushrooms. It was the only piece of information he didn't have. I think he went back to Villa Gesell a couple of days before my parents' wedding anniversary and scattered the poisonous fungi amongst the edible ones, but with the base missing, so there was no way of distinguishing between them. *He removed the bases.* And before leaving he made sure he left a few buried in leaf litter, in case there was a forensic examination afterwards.'

I tried to picture Kloster – the Kloster who appeared in the papers – engaged in such horticultural skulduggery.

'I suppose it's possible, though it sounds a little complicated. It seems more like the kind of murder he'd devise for one of his novels,' I said. But at the same time, and perhaps precisely because of that, I had to admit to myself that it didn't seem all that unreasonable. 'But how could he have managed it with your boyfriend?'

Luciana looked at me, eyes shining, as if she were about to confide a magical formula that she alone in the world had discovered.

'*The cup of coffee with milk.* That was the key. I

woke up with a start early one morning and it came to me: I remembered the row with Ramiro over the waitress and how my coffee – the one with milk – was always cold. I'd thought it was petty spitefulness on her part when in fact, with hindsight, I realised it was just something all waiters do: to save herself a trip she sometimes waited for another order to be put on her tray, together with ours. As she was the only one waiting on the tables outside, it also quite often happened that orders were left at the bar for a minute, until she went back inside. Kloster was sitting right there, where the owner of the bar placed the trays with the cups. And he knew very well that I always had milk in my coffee, which meant he knew that the black coffee had to be Ramiro's. He simply waited for the first rough day, so that it would look like an accident.'

'Do you mean he poisoned your boyfriend's coffee?'

'I don't think it was poison; that would have been too risky. He must have known that there'd be a routine post-mortem afterwards. I think he chose a substance that pathologists wouldn't automatically be looking for, something that could cause arrhythmia, or the beginnings of suffocation, or maybe massive cramps. He was a swimmer, so he'd know, say, that a sudden potassium deficiency causes cramps. It could simply have been a powerful diuretic. At first, I didn't realise exactly how it had all happened. I thought I'd have to convince Ramiro's parents to have his body exhumed, but now I think that would only have made things worse. I'm sure he planned this too: nothing unusual would be detected and he'd be above suspicion once again.'

'Did you tell anyone about this?'

Her face darkened. 'My brother. That morning, when it all suddenly became clear to me, I went to see him. He was working a shift at the hospital. I think I was a little overwrought: I hadn't slept for several nights since the funeral. My hands were trembling and I was almost feverish with excitement. I showed Bruno the passage in the Bible and told him about my suing Kloster, and the death of Kloster's daughter, the Cainites and sevenfold vengeance. I explained how I thought he'd planned the deaths. But I got a little muddled: I couldn't explain it as clearly as I'd understood it. At a certain point I realised he was no longer listening, but was watching me with the eyes of a doctor. He looked genuinely alarmed. He saw that my hands were shaking and asked how long I'd gone without sleep. He told me to wait there and left the room for a moment. The book he'd been reading was lying on the desk. There was something horribly familiar about the cover so I turned it round: *it was one of Kloster's novels.* I think at that moment I collapsed. My brother reappeared with a psychiatrist who was on duty, but I wouldn't answer any of her questions. I knew what they were thinking. The psychiatrist said they'd give me something to help me sleep. She used a horrible patronising voice, as if she were explaining something to a child. My own brother gave me the injection. My own brother, who was reading one of Kloster's novels during his shift.'

'If it was the novel that came out that year, I don't find it too surprising: it was an even bigger hit than his previous one. It would have been hard to find someone who *wasn't* reading it.'

'That's just it. That's why I was so devastated. I saw how perfect his plan was. It wasn't surprising – it was quite natural – that everything should go his way. It's what I said to you at the beginning: this was maybe the most cunning part. His name was everywhere, he'd become a public figure, moving in circles beyond the reach of mere mortals. So when I tried to point the finger at him everyone looked at me as my brother had, and rushed for psychiatrists.'

'But after you were given the tranquilliser . . .'

'They gave me another one, and another one. To put it simply, it was like a sleep cure. Until I realised what I had to do if I wanted them to stop drugging me and get out of that place. I just had to make sure I never mentioned the K word.'

A tear of frustration ran down her cheek. She pulled off the latex gloves. Her hands, now reddened, were trembling even more than before.

'Well, I think I've told you the worst. But I wanted you to know everything. I was in hospital for two weeks and by the time I got out I'd learned my lesson: I never mentioned this to anyone again. More time passed – a whole year, then another. But I wasn't fooled this time. I knew it was part of his plan that the deaths should be spaced out. Perhaps that was the worst part: the waiting. I stopped seeing my friends; I became isolated. I didn't want anyone near me. I didn't know where the next blow would come from. I was mainly terrified for Valentina. She was my responsibility by then as my brother had moved to a flat of his own. I hated leaving her alone even for a minute. The waiting that stretched on, living in suspense, the *delay* – it was unbearable. I tried to keep track of him in the papers, to find out the itineraries of his journeys in the news, where he could be. I only had a few days' respite whenever I knew he was out of the country. Until finally it happened. I got a phone call from the police superintendent: a burglar had broken into my brother's flat and killed him. My brother, who thought I'd lost my mind, was now dead. That was all the superintendent said but the gruesome details were already on the news. My brother hadn't put up a fight, but the killer had been especially vicious, as if there was something more between them. He'd had a gun but had used his bare hands. He broke both my brother's arms and gouged out his eyes. I think he did something even more horrible afterwards to the body, but I could never bring myself to read the pathologist's report through to the end. When the police caught the man he still had my brother's blood on his face.'

'I remember. I remember it quite clearly,' I said, amazed that I'd never made the connection. 'He was a prisoner in a maximum security prison, and he got out to commit burglaries with the guards' permission. Well, at least here it's obvious it wasn't Kloster.'

'*It was Kloster*,' she said, eyes blazing.

For a moment it all felt unreal. Her mouth was twisted angrily. She'd spoken with absolute conviction, with the dark determination of a fanatic, who will brook no contradiction. But a moment later she was crying quietly, pausing now and then as if the effort of having reached this point had exhausted her. She took a handkerchief from her bag, wringing it helplessly after wiping her eyes. Once she'd recovered, her voice was again controlled, oddly calm and distant.

'At the time, my brother was working in the prison hospital wing. Apparently this is where he met the convict's wife. Unfortunately he became involved with her. They thought they were safe because the husband was serving a life sentence. They never dreamed that he had an arrangement with the guards to get out and burgle homes. It was a huge scandal in the prison service when it all came to light. The Internal Investigations

Department had to carry out a detailed inquiry. That's when they discovered the letters. Someone had been sending the prisoner anonymous letters, giving details of his wife's meetings with my brother. The letters were in the court record so I was able to see them. The handwriting had been disguised. And there were deliberate spelling and grammatical mistakes. But I took dictation from Kloster for almost a year and he couldn't fool me. It was his style – precise, calculating, full of humiliating details. Intended line by line to drive the man crazy. The scenes . . . the *physical* scenes were probably made up, but the letters gave very precise descriptions of the bar where they met, the clothes she wore each time, how the two of them made fun of him. Those letters were the real murder weapon. And whoever wrote them was the true murderer.'

'Did you tell the police any of this at the time?'

'I asked to speak to the officer in charge of the case, Superintendent Ramoneda. At first he was very pleasant and seemed willing to listen. I told him everything: about my suing Kloster, Ramiro's death, my parents' poisoning, the clues that it was Kloster who wrote the anonymous letters. He listened without saying a word, but I realised he didn't like the direction things might go in if he decided to take me seriously. After all, for them it was an open-and-shut case. I think he was afraid he might be accused, in the midst of all the scandal, of wanting to absolve the prison service. He asked if I understood the gravity of my accusation and the absolute absence of proof in all that I'd told him. He took down Kloster's details anyway and said he'd send one of his men to speak to him. A couple of days later I got a call summoning me back to his office. I could tell immediately that something had changed. His tone was both fatherly and slightly threatening. He said that because it was such a delicate matter and there was so much at stake he'd decided to go and see Kloster himself – he had to follow every lead, however absurd. Kloster, he said, had been very courteous – he was about to leave for a reception at the French embassy but had made time. He didn't tell me about the interview itself but it was obvious that Kloster had impressed him. I've no doubt they ended up talking about his novels. Before I could say anything he produced a sheet of paper in my handwriting and laid it on the desk. I recognised it at once: it was the letter I sent Kloster after my parents died. A letter in which I asked his forgiveness for having sued him.'

'You sent Kloster a letter of apology? You didn't mention it.'

'It was when I came out of hospital. I was confused and terrified. I didn't want to spend the rest of my life waiting for everyone close to me to die. I thought that if I asked for forgiveness humbly, pleaded and took all the blame, he'd stop. It was a mistake made in a moment of desperation. But when I tried to explain this to the super-intendent he took out another document: the admission form for the psychiatric clinic where I was given the sleep cure. He said he'd had to make inquiries about me too. From his tone, he made it clear he thought he had my measure and wasn't prepared to waste any more time on me. He asked if I realised that with the same lack of proof somebody sufficiently imaginative, or deranged, might also accuse *me*. Then he went back to a fatherly tone and advised me to accept that my boyfriend's death had simply been a careless accident, my parents' a tragedy, and there was nothing more to it. They'd caught my brother's killer and this was indeed quite another matter: surely I hadn't forgotten that they'd caught the brute with my brother's blood around his mouth? Did I want them to let him go and instead pursue a writer awarded the Grand Cross of the Légion d'honneur with whom I'd had a personal problem of some sort several years ago? He stood up and said he couldn't help me any further but there was a public prosecutor on the case if I wanted to take my stories to him.'

'But you didn't,' I said.

She looked defeated. 'No, I didn't,' she said.

She lapsed into a long helpless silence, as if now that she'd told me everything she had retreated further into herself. She sat hunched in the armchair, hands with fin-gers interlaced in her lap, jerking her head and shoulders back and forth in small compulsive movements. She looked on the verge of shivering.

'Don't you have any other relatives who could help you?'

She shook her head, slowly, resignedly. 'All that's left of my family is my grandmother Margarita. She's been in an old people's home for years. And my sister, Valentina, who's still at school.'

'What happened after that? It's been a few years since your brother died, hasn't it?'

'Four. He's letting time pass again. These periods are torture. I almost never leave the flat, and I watch Valentina constantly. I've become obsessive about cross-roads, and locks, and turning off the gas. But I can't control Valentina completely any more. I can't stop her going out with her friends sometimes. My God, some-times I even follow her without her knowing, to make sure he's not after her. I only visit my grandmother once a week, on Saturday afternoons, but I've left written instructions not to allow in any visitors except Valentina and me. I'm scared he'll get in there under a pretext, in disguise . . .'

'But from what you've said he seems to prefer indirect methods. Or do you think he'd risk doing something himself?'

'I just don't know. It's unbearable not knowing what'll come next. I've tried to take precautions, but you

can't take every single possible precaution. It's so difficult . . . I hadn't seen him again for all this time and even
though I never forgot for a moment, the waiting had
come to seem unreal, even to me. As if only I was per-
petuating it, because only I *knew*. And him. Until I saw
him again yesterday. I think it was carelessness on his
part. I think I've got a slight advantage for the first time.
Or maybe not, maybe he's so confident that he let me see
him, the way he did at the cemetery. I'd just been to visit
my grandmother and I went into the antiques shop below
the old people's home. At one point I looked out and saw
him standing across the street, staring up at the windows
of the home. The traffic lights were red, but he just stood
at the kerb, apparently examining the row of windows or
an architectural detail. He didn't see me. He stared up at
the building for a few moments, then walked away without crossing the road.'

'Is it an old building? Maybe he genuinely was admir-
ing one of the stained glass windows or the mouldings on
the balconies?'

'Maybe. I expect that's what he'd say. But my grandmother has one of the rooms looking out on to the
street.'

'I see. And this was yesterday. Is that why you decided
to call me?'

'There's that, and something else. It would almost be
funny, if I could still find anything funny. My sister's in

her final year at school and about a month ago her literature teacher decided they should read a novel by a contemporary author. Of all the writers in Argentina, guess who she chose?'

'I didn't know Kloster was recommended reading in schools now. I expect teenagers find his novels pretty stirring.'

'Yes, that's the right word, if you want to put it tactfully. Valentina was completely gripped by the book – I think she read it in a couple of days. I've never seen her so absorbed by a novel. Over the next few weeks she devoured everything by Kloster in the school library. And then . . . she persuaded her teacher to ask him to come and give a talk to the class. Last night she told me Kloster has agreed. She's thrilled that she's going to get to meet him. And she said something that made my blood run cold: she's going to try to interview him for the school magazine.'

'But haven't you told her anything all these years? Doesn't she know . . .'

'No. I've never told her. She was only a child when I worked for Kloster and to her he was just a nameless writer I went to work for every morning. She has no inkling of any of the rest of it. I wanted her to have a normal life, as far as possible. I never dreamed she'd jump into the wolf's mouth herself. Yesterday, when she told me, I thought I'd start screaming in front of her. I

didn't sleep all night. And suddenly I remembered you.'
She looked at me, and I felt she was extending an imploring hand to me. 'I remembered that you're a writer too. I thought you could speak to him. You could speak for me.' She burst into anguished sobs and, as if she no longer cared about holding back, she said, almost screaming: 'I don't want to die. I don't want to die like this, without even knowing why. I just want you to find out.'

I suppose I should have put my arms round her, but I couldn't bring myself to. I sat frozen, terrified by her violent sobbing, waiting for her to calm down.

'You're not going to die,' I said. 'Nobody else is going to die.'

'I just want to know why,' she said through her tears. 'Speak to him and ask him why. Please,' she begged, 'will you do this for me?'

4

Once I was back out in the piercing cold night air, I saw the problem, or set of problems, I'd got myself into. So had I believed Luciana? Strange as I find it now, as I walked home through the last traces of that Sunday, to some extent I had believed her, just as you believe in the revolution while you're reading *The Communist Manifesto* or *Ten Days that Shook the World*. At any rate I'd believed her enough to make that stupid promise. The more I thought about it, the harder it seemed to keep. I didn't know Kloster personally; I'd never even seen him. Ten years earlier, when I wrote for various literary supplements, at a time when I went from literary gatherings to book launches, from round tables to newspaper offices, it would have been impossible not to meet him had he deigned to show his face at such events. But during those years Kloster's persistent non-appearance had become legendary, and was, I assumed, another expression of his lofty contempt for us. Some of us had even toyed with the idea that Kloster didn't in fact exist, that he was the joint invention of several writers, like mathematicians' Nicolas Bourbaki, or of a pair of writers, secret lovers who couldn't sign their names together. The couple of rather hazy photographs reproduced for years on the flaps of his books could easily have been faked. We joked and speculated and compared, but Kloster was too different, light years from the galaxy of Argentinian writers, like a cold star in the distance. And in the years that followed, when Kloster underwent his spectacular transformation and was frenetically everywhere, I'd made my own journey to the end of the night. On my return – if, that is, I had returned – I'd preferred to keep away from everything and everyone, shutting myself up like a phobic within the four walls of my apartment. I'd never returned to the literary scene and now only went out for walks or to give a class.

If Kloster and I had utterly failed to coincide, something separated us even more. When Kloster had done something unforgivable – have his first big success – the machinery of petty resentments in the literary world had cranked into action against him. What had once been a well-guarded secret, passed quietly with bewildered admiration amongst connoisseurs of the obscure, was now in full view, at the same democratic price as the work of any other Argentinian author, and, in the great wave of recognition, Kloster's earlier novels reappeared. Ordinary readers in their thousands suddenly purchased those early books, which had once circulated like passwords among the cognoscenti. It could mean only one thing: Kloster couldn't be as good as we'd thought and we had, quickly, to backtrack and shoot him down. To my shame, I was part of the firing squad, with an article full of irony about the writer I most admired. It had been just after Luciana stopped working for me and I was still feeling hurt at the thought – the conviction – that she'd gone back to him. And though almost ten years had passed and the article had appeared in an obscure journal that now no longer even existed, I was only too familiar with the tangled web of literary intrigue: someone had no doubt placed it in front of him at some stage, and if he'd read it, and was even half as vindictive as Luciana believed, he would not have forgiven me.

I couldn't even contemplate phoning him and saying my name. He'd hang up before I could get a sentence out. I thought of increasingly crazy possibilities: turn up at his door, engineer a meeting in the street, give a false name and pretend to be a journalist. But even if I cleared the first hurdle, even if I managed to enter Kloster's fortress of fame and we exchanged a few words, how on earth could I talk to him about Luciana, broach the real subject, without the conversation's ending before it began? I fell asleep, annoyed with myself for having got into a mess that wasn't mine and that I was desperate to get out of. Why did I say yes when everything inside me was saying no, I wondered again. We always treat women too well, as Queneau might have said. Even their ghosts, I thought in the oppressive darkness of my bedroom, unable to picture the face of the real Luciana from ten years ago.

I awoke the next day feeling as if I'd had a drunken night out but that, despite the hangover, my senses and my equanimity had been returned to me. In the warm, familiar sunlight coming through the window, I felt myself swing towards scepticism, and the suspicion that I'd been ensnared in a series of careful lies told by an apparition from the past. Desperate for caffeine, I went out to have breakfast in a bar, and as I reviewed Luciana's story in search of contradictions and errors I realised, with that same lucid calm, that if I had now decided to doubt what I'd heard, it was mainly to get out of this ludicrous mission.

I didn't have classes that Monday, but I had to go to El Bajo to collect the tickets for my flight on Wednesday to Salinas, where I was to give a postgraduate course at the Universidad del Oeste. The offices of one of the newspapers for which I'd once written reviews were also in El Bajo. I decided that before doing anything it would be worth consulting the archives to confirm the most salient facts, at least.

When I got to the old building by the river, I too felt like a ghost haunting a place that no longer existed. Like a cathedral under restoration, the façade was unrecognisable, hidden behind scaffolding. I searched for the entrance amongst temporary signs and boardwalks. Someone who had come outside to smoke greeted me from a distance without much surprise or enthusiasm; I returned the greeting automatically, not entirely sure who it was. Inside the receptionists were new, but the basement where the archives were kept was unchanged, as if it was too difficult to shift the past. I went down the stairs and again breathed in the smell of damp exuded by the peeling walls, and felt the sagging floorboards creak beneath my feet, betraying my presence. I was alone down there and assumed the librarian had gone for lunch. I searched the shelves myself. The first three deaths had taken place before newspapers were digitised but I soon found the box files containing the copies for each year. I almost missed the first item as it occupied only a tiny space at the bottom of a page. Headed 'Lifeguard Drowns', the article didn't mention Luciana. It simply stated that the rescue operation had been unsuccessful, and that cold and exhaustion had caused the young life-guard to suffer massive cramps, despite his being very fit. That was all, with no further details the following day. I supposed that no one in the resort wanted to publicise a drowning at the start of the season.

The item about her parents' poisoning, on the other hand, near the end of the next box file, took up over half a page. There was a rather blurry photograph of a tree with some fungi beneath it, and a comparative diagram of *Amanita phalloides* and an edible mushroom. An arrow indicated where the volva had become detached, as Luciana had explained. The article mentioned that the couple had three children, but that none of them was with them at the house at the time. It didn't give their names, and Luciana's surname was so common that I wouldn't have registered the item even if I'd read it back then. There was a slightly shorter article the following day, explaining that a search of the little wood had confirmed the presence of the poisonous species. It mentioned how spores could be carried considerable distances on the wind and warned of the dangers of amateur mushroom gathering.

I took the articles to the photocopier, and as I inserted coins and watched the beam of light pass over the pages I had the feeling that an idea, as yet unformed, was trying to emerge, like an elusive animal lurking – about to brush past, about to flee – in that silent basement. On impulse

I returned to the rows of files and searched for reports of the fourth death. The progression here was in reverse: the story began with a tiny item lost in the Police Reports page, but then, as the political implications became apparent, it had taken up more and more space until it featured on the front page. I read the first day's article, as yet without photographs. The killer had apparently been waiting for the doctor late at night, at the entrance to his building, and had held him up at gunpoint. Luciana's brother hadn't put up a fight, perhaps believing it was just a mugging. They'd gone up in the lift to his apartment. Neighbours had heard a terrible commotion and the doctor shouting. Someone had called the police. The door to the apartment was open and the man's revolver was in plain view on a shelf, as if he'd put it down there as soon as he entered. The doctor's body lay in the middle of the sitting room, his eyes gouged out and a huge wound on his neck, possibly caused by a bite. The police had found the killer on the roof of the building, his mouth smeared with blood. When they managed to unclench his fist they found he was gripping the doctor's eyeballs, crushed to a pulp. In his statement he said he had wanted to throw them in his wife's face before killing her.

I looked for the next day's paper. The story now occupied over half a page. It turned out that the arrested man had already been sentenced to life in a high security prison, but nobody could explain how he'd got out. There was a photograph of him looking straight at the camera, eyes empty of all expression, probably his police mug shot: a wide forehead, bald with narrow strips of hair above his ears, a sharp nose, plain ordinary features that gave no hint of murder or butchery. The post-mortem had revealed a few more details. The murderer had used only his hands and teeth; the victim had barely resisted, failing to land a single blow. The killer was famous in prison for letting his nails grow long, and had already blinded another inmate in a fight. It hadn't been established whether the doctor had still been conscious when he'd had his eyes gouged out. In any case the cause of death was severing of the jugular vein. The report also stated that the doctor had been having an affair with the convict's wife, whom he'd met when she was visiting her husband in prison, but there was no mention of the anonymous letters Luciana had told me about.

I looked at the next day's paper. The story had now reached the front page. Apparently the inmate hadn't escaped, he had been let out by guards to commit a burglary. The Ministry of the Interior had intervened and the head of the prison service was expected to resign imminently. The investigation had changed hands and was now being conducted by the same Superintendent Ramoneda that Luciana had mentioned. Even so, as I read this article – by far the longest – I felt that the trail was fading; that, as in the children's game, I was getting cold. No, this definitely wasn't what I thought I'd glimpsed. There was something earlier which I had missed again as I read. I took the first day's article to the photocopier and then I went to one of the desks and set out all three copied stories. I read them again, one after the other. Almost nothing seemed to connect them, other than Luciana's account. The dates were unevenly spaced: the first two incidents had taken place within a year, but the third had occurred three years later, and now four years had elapsed since anything had happened. There seemed, at any rate, to be a slowing of the pace of killing. Nor was there any obvious pattern linking them, discernible 'from the outside'. There was even an aesthetic inconsistency: if the first two cases were to a certain extent reminiscent of the kind of subtle murder Kloster devised in his novels, the third – brutal, bloody – was quite unlike his style, his literary style at least. Though it might, of course, be part of the plan, and an obvious precaution for some of the deaths to be very different from those in his books. I recalled Luciana's anxious voice the first time she called me: *nobody knows, nobody realises.* No, nobody knew, nobody realised, though all three cases had been in the papers, though the deaths were there, in plain sight, and one of them had caused quite a scandal. But was there really nothing to link them? A moment earlier, I thought I'd seen something, something that now eluded me but was nevertheless still there. Suddenly I thought I had the answer, though it didn't seem to be of much use. It was something Luciana had said when describing her brother's death. With his *bare hands*. The article on the first day also mentioned it: the killer had put down his gun and used only his hands and teeth. I sensed that this was it but, as if the scarcely glimpsed figure had once again melted away, I still couldn't fully see the connection. And what significance, if any, did it have? Even if I accepted that Kloster was behind the deaths, even if I accepted that he had written the anonymous letters, of which there was no mention in the articles, there didn't seem to be any way that he or anyone else could have foreseen that the killer would put down his gun and use only his hands. Or was there some prison code I was unaware of by which killing face to face, with bare hands, was the payback for infidelity? I resolved to find out. Anyway, simply by following Luciana's brother, Kloster could have found out that he was having an affair with the convict's wife, but it was much more unlikely that he would also have known that the prisoner, serving a life sentence, was allowed out to commit burglaries.

Every time I went over it, the case against Kloster seemed convoluted and unbelievable. But then, as I knew, the plots of Kloster's novels also seemed convoluted and unbelievable, until you reached the last page. It was precisely because the case against Kloster had something excessive, something disproportionate, about it that I couldn't discount it entirely.

I folded the pages and left the building, without dropping in to the editorial office to say hello to my erstwhile colleagues. Actually I was afraid there would be no one left that I knew. I walked home, hoping that during the walk I'd come up with a reasonable – or convincing – excuse for calling Kloster.

In the lift on the way up to my apartment, I heard the phone ring one last time before stopping. Nobody phoned nowadays and when I opened the door, in the silence amplified by that last ring, the apartment felt emptier than ever. I was under no illusions: I knew exactly who was calling and what she wanted to know. I reflected that she was right, at least, about the grey rug: I'd have to find the energy at some stage to get a new one. I went to the kitchen to make coffee, but just as I was rinsing out a cup the phone rang again. I wondered how early she'd started ringing like that, at five-minute intervals. It was, indeed, Luciana.

'Have you spoken to him?'

Her voice was anxious, but there was also something slightly imperious in her tone, as if the favour she'd wrung from me in tears the night before had, by morning, become a duty I had to report on.

'No, not yet. Actually I don't even have his number. I was thinking of calling my editor now . . .'

'I've got it,' she said. 'I'll give it to you.'

'Is it the number at the house you used to go to?'

'No. He had to move out of there after his divorce.'

I wondered how she'd managed to get hold of the new number. But I realised, then, that Luciana had to know his new address. How else could she have sent him the letter? If indeed Kloster was secretly watching her every step, the watching, it seemed, was mutual. She spoke again, her impatience barely contained, as if she felt she'd left me no excuse.

'So will you call him now?'

'The thing is, I still can't think how to go about it. I don't even know him. So, calling out of the blue, to talk to him about something like this . . . Anyway,' I said, 'I once wrote a rather unpleasant article about him. If by any chance he read it I don't think he'll let me get out a single word.'

As I listed excuse after excuse, I felt more and more contemptible. But she stopped me.

'There is one way,' she said darkly. 'Something you could say if all else fails. After all, he must think I've completely lost my mind over these years. You could say you've had a conversation with me that's worried you. You have to talk to him, because you get the impression that I'm desperate. I feel cornered and even made you believe that I might try something against him. I mean, I've thought of it a thousand times: *pre-empt his next move*. It would be self-defence. I would have done it already if I only dared, or could think of a way, like him, of not getting caught. When he hears his life's in danger, he'll want to know more.'

I listened with a shiver of revulsion at her obsession, but had to admit that it was a better idea than any I'd come up with so far.

'Fine,' I said. 'I'll keep it in mind as a last resort.'

'So will you call him now? Please,' she said, her voice faltering. 'I don't know how much time we have left. I'm sure he's about to try something.'

'Of course I will. I promised, didn't I?' I said. 'I'll call now. I'll speak to him and we'll sort this out.'

I hung up and sat staring with annoyance at the phone number I'd just jotted down, as if it were a note left by a stranger that was now throbbing and ticking insistently. I hadn't had any scrap paper to hand, so I'd written it down on the lined pad where I made notes for my novels, beneath a list of provisional titles. I suddenly knew what I had to do, and it seemed so obvious it almost made me smile. Of course. Of course. What could be more natural? It was the only thing that Kloster would believe: I'd tell him I was about to start a novel.

5

'Kloster?'

'Yes?'

The voice was deep, rough, a little impatient, as if I was interrupting him in the middle of something.

'Campari gave me your number,' I said, prepared to lie as many times as necessary. I said my name and held my breath. It felt risky, but he gave no sign of recognition. 'My first two novels were published by him,' I added, not sure if this would help.

'Ah yes, of course: the author of *Deception*.'

'*Desertion*,' I corrected him, deflated, and added defensively: 'That was my first novel.'

'*Desertion*, of course, now I remember. Strange title, rather extreme for a first novel. I remember wondering what you'd call your second – *With my Tail Between my Legs* perhaps? At the time you seemed only to have read Lyotard: you wanted to give up before you'd started. Although there was also something towards the end of *Lost Illusions*, wasn't there? I'm glad you went on to write a second. That's the paradox for champions of renunciation, of limits, ends: they then want to write another novel. I'd have put money on your becoming a critic. I think I saw your name on a review at one stage. A review full of the usual jargon. And I thought I was right.'

So had he read my article about his novels? I couldn't tell for sure from his tone but at least he hadn't hung up.

'I did write reviews for a couple of years,' I said. 'But I never stopped writing novels. My second, *The Random Men*, came out the same year as your *Day of the Dead*, though it didn't do as well. And I've written another two since then,' I said, offended despite myself that he knew so little about my work.

'I didn't know. I suppose I should do more to keep up. Anyway, I'm pleased for you: the prophet of abandonment has become a prolific author. But I'm sure you didn't call to talk about your books, or mine.'

'Actually, I did,' I said. 'I'm calling because I'm about to begin writing a novel based on a true story.'

'A *true* story?' he said mockingly. 'It really is all change. I thought you despised realism and were only interested in who knows what daring stylistic experiments.'

'You're right,' I said, prepared to take the blows. 'This is quite unlike anything I've ever written. It's a story I've been told and I want to set it down exactly, almost like a history, or a report. Anyway, it sounds so unlikely that no one would believe it was true. Except, maybe, the people involved. That's why I'm calling,' I said, and waited for his reaction.

'I'm one of the people involved?' He sounded amused and still a little incredulous.

'I'd say you're the central character.'

There was silence at the other end, as if Kloster now knew what was coming and was preparing to play a different game.

'I see,' he said. 'And what is this story you've been told?'

'It's about a series of unexplained deaths, surrounding a single person.'

'A *crime* story? So you're moving into my field now? What I don't understand,' he said after a moment, 'is how I can be the central character. Unless I'm the next victim?' he asked in mock alarm. 'I know some writers of your generation would like to see me dead, but I've always assumed it was metaphorical. I hope they're not prepared to take action.'

'No, you're not the victim. You're the one behind the deaths. At least, that's what the person who told me about it believes.' And I said Luciana's full name. Kloster gave a brief, unpleasant laugh.

'I was wondering how long you'd take to get round to her. So the Lady of Shalott is back on the attack. I suppose I should be grateful: last time, she sent a policeman so she's getting a bit subtler with her envoys. I can't believe anyone is still prepared to listen to her. But of course you were involved with her, weren't you?'

'I hadn't seen her for ten years. Actually, I'm not sure yet how much I believe her. But enough to want to write about it. Obviously I wouldn't want to publish without hearing your side of the story.'

'My side of it . . . Strange you should say that. I've been writing a story myself, with the same characters. But I'm sure it'll be quite different from yours.'

This seemed like a lucky piece of news that I might be able to use. After all, there's nothing more worrying for a writer than finding out someone else has got his eye on your subject. I had to play my cards carefully.

'Could we meet?' I said. 'Any day you can spare a minute of your time. I could show you what I've written so far, based on what she's told me. If you explain why I shouldn't believe her, I'll give up on the whole idea. I wouldn't want to publish anything that might disparage you unfairly.'

As usual, I'd gone too far.

'Put like that,' said Kloster coldly, 'it sounds almost like blackmail. I've had to deal with blackmail from that girl once before. Or hasn't she mentioned it? I don't have to convince you of anything. I don't owe anyone an explanation. If you believe a madwoman, you're the one with a problem, not me.' His voice was growing louder and I thought he might be about to hang up.

'No, no, of course not,' I said placatingly. 'Please, I'm not her envoy – I'm not involved with her in any way. She's come to see me after ten years, and she did appear to be a little disturbed.'

'A little disturbed . . . You're being generous. Well, if that's clear, I don't have a problem with meeting you. I can tell you a few things myself. And there's something I'd like to ask you, something I'd like to include in my novel. But we can discuss it when we meet. Do you have my address?'

I said yes.

'Fine. I'll expect you here tomorrow at six.'

6

'What do I think?' said Kloster, reading the last of my pages. With distaste he pushed aside the small stack that had grown in front of him, as if he couldn't bear to look at it. He leaned back in his chair, stretching his arms above his head, palms touching. Despite the cold outside, he was wearing only a short-sleeved T-shirt, and his long bare arms looked like two triangles suspended in the air.

I hadn't slept the previous night and didn't feel up to the coming confrontation. I'd worked against the clock setting up my little sham. I'd tried to record Luciana's story just as she had recounted it, from the moment she arrived at my apartment. I had included my own questions, and all her pauses and hesitations, even the sentences she left hanging. But I had omitted my thoughts about her and also – especially – my reaction to her appearance, and my doubts about her mental state. All that appeared on paper was the bald sequence of lines of dialogue, the to and fro of our voices, just as if they'd been transcribed. I'd worked all night with hypnotic intensity induced by endlessly rerunning the same memory: Luciana's face in the deepening gloom of my living room and her terror as she cried out that she didn't want to die. I'd revised and corrected, details disappearing and reappearing intermittently and ever more slowly, until at last, at dawn, I printed out about twenty pages. This was the bait with which I arrived, at six o'clock in the evening, at Kloster's house.

I rang the bell and stood for a moment in awe before an imposing iron gate. The buzzer sounded, admitting me to the entrance hall, and I saw a great marble staircase, bronze statues, antique mirrors, with a stab of admiration close to envy. I couldn't help wondering how many books you had to sell to pay for such a house in an area like this.

Kloster, waiting for me at the top of the stairs, held out his hand and looked at me for a moment as if making sure we had never met before. He was taller than I had imagined from his photographs, and though he must have been over fifty there was something youthful and vigorous in the upright figure, almost a flaunting of his athleticism, that made one think of the long-distance swimmer first and then the writer. But despite the still powerful body, his face was a ruin, cruelly sunken, as if the flesh had withdrawn, exposing the sharp edges of his bones, and the cold blue eyes, fixing me with uncomfortable intensity, had retreated with it. He shook my hand briskly, simultaneously motioning towards the library. There had been no hint of a smile, nor the standard exchange of trivialities, as if he wanted to make it clear from the start that I wasn't entirely welcome. But this initial rejection of conventional courtesy actually made things easier: neither of us was under any illusions. Nevertheless, as he indicated an armchair, he offered to get me a coffee and I accepted, though I had been drinking cup after cup since morning to keep myself awake. As soon as he disappeared down one of the corridors I got up and looked around. The library was impressive, with shelves almost to the ceiling. But the effect wasn't oppressive as two large windows provided a break from the book-lined walls. There was another armchair in a corner with a standard lamp beside it, where Kloster no doubt sat to read. I walked along the bookshelves, running my finger over some of the titles. In a gap between encyclopaedias, neither hidden nor prominently displayed, I saw the Grand Cross of the Légion d'honneur with its tricolour ribbon. I went over to the narrow glass-fronted bookcase between the windows. Here Kloster kept all the different editions of his own books, together with their translations into dozens of languages. Again I felt a dart of envy, sharper this time, the same shameful feeling which I knew, over and above Luciana, was what had made me attack Kloster in that contemptible article that could be summed up in a mute complaint: *why him and not me?* All I can say in my defence is that it was hard, standing before that bookcase, not to feel like a hazy dispossessed Enoch Soames. Opposite the corridor down which Kloster had disappeared there was another, narrower corridor off the library, leading perhaps to staff quarters or to his study. In the dim early evening light the corridor was in gloom but I could just see that the walls were lined with framed photographs. Irresistibly drawn, I went to look at the nearest of these: it showed a pretty little girl of about three or four with tousled hair, wearing a polka dot dress, standing on a chair and reaching up towards Kloster. The writer looked transformed – or should I say transported? – smiling expectantly, waiting for the little outstretched hand to touch his face. Part of the photo appeared to have been cut off at an angle, as if a figure had been excised from the scene. I heard steps returning from the kitchen and went back to the armchair. Kloster placed two large mugs on the glass coffee table and muttered something about there being no sugar in the house. He sat down opposite me and immediately picked up the transparent plastic folder in which I'd placed the pages.

'So this is the story,' he said.

And for about forty minutes that was all. He took the pages from the folder and set them in a little stack on the desk. He picked them up one by one to read them, forming a second pile as he set them face down. I was expecting him to object, become angry, even throw them aside or tear them up, but he read on in silence, looking increasingly gloomy, as if, as he read, he were returning to an unbearable past that was now again clutching at him with long ghostly fingers. Once or twice he shook his head incredulously and when he was finished he stared into space for a long time, still not speaking, as if he'd forgotten I was there. He didn't even look at me when I asked what he thought, but simply echoed my question, as if it had come not from another person but from inside himself.

'What do I think? An astonishing clinical account. Like those Oliver Sacks records about his patients. The extraction of the stone of madness. I suppose I should be grateful you've changed my name in the text. But the one you've chosen,' and he pronounced the name contemptuously, 'how on earth did you settle on it?'

'I wanted a name that evoked something closed, like a monastery,' I attempted to explain. I never would have dreamed that, after all the accusations he'd just read, this was what might bother him.

'Something closed, I see. So who would you be? The open Overt?'

I found this doubly surprising. I would never have imagined that Kloster had read Henry James, much less that he would fling the name of one of his characters at me out of the blue, like a taunt. It could only mean one thing: Kloster had read my series of articles on James. And if he'd read those, he must have seen my attack on him, which had appeared in the same journal, and he was now playing cat and mouse with me. I said only the first part – that I would never have suspected he might be interested in Henry James. He seemed offended by this.

'Why not? Because in my novels there are never fewer than ten deaths and in James's the most that ever happens is that someone doesn't get married? As a writer yourself, you shouldn't be confused by trivia such as murders and marriages. What is it that counts in a crime novel? Definitely not the facts, or the succession of dead bodies. It's what you should read *behind* them, the conjectures, the possible explanations. And isn't James's central theme precisely that: what each character conjectures? The possible reach of every action, the abyss of consequences and bifurcations. "Man is no more than the series of his actions," Hegel once wrote. Yet James constructed his entire oeuvre in the interstices between actions, between lines of dialogue, in characters' second and third intentions, in the agony of hesitations and calculations and strategies that precedes every action.'

'You might also say that in James's novels marriage is a form of murder,' I ventured.

'Of course: a kidnapping followed by death,' he agreed, as if he'd never thought of it like that and was surprised that I had uttered an entire sentence with which he agreed. 'Strange that we should be talking about James,' he said, and his tone, for the first time, was slightly less hostile, 'because it was a book of his that began everything: the *Notebooks*.' He pointed to one of the uppermost shelves. 'If you've ever had a look at them, you'll remember the preface by Leon Edel. I'd never read a biography of James. As a rule I'm wary of writers' biographies, but in that introduction I found something very interesting: at a certain point James stopped writing by hand and started dictating his novels to typists and stenographers. I was having a similar problem at the time. Not exactly tendonitis – that would hardly be likely in my case. But I've always found it easier to think on my feet and I could never sit at my desk for long. I'd pace the room, then sit down to write a few lines, but if I wanted to continue I had to get up again almost immediately. It made progress painfully slow. When I read the preface to the *Notebooks* I suddenly found the solution. That's how I came to hire Luciana.'

'How did you find her?' I asked. I had always wondered.

'I put an ad in the paper. It was an easy choice: she

was the only applicant who could spell. Of course I was struck immediately by how pretty she was, but I didn't think it would be a problem – she wasn't my type. To put it bluntly, she had no tits. But I'm sure you know that better than I do,' he shot at me. 'Anyway, it seemed ideal: as I said, I wanted to get more work done, not less.'

'So none of what she said about her relationship with you actually happened?' I asked. At this he looked annoyed again.

'It did, but quite differently from the way she describes it. That's why I wanted to tell you a couple of things. At first everything went well. Incredibly well. Luciana passed my ex-wife's initial inspection. Mercedes had a practised eye for spotting a potential threat in any woman who came near me. I think she discounted Luciana because she looked so young. Or maybe because she had that thin teenager's body and the look of a conscientious schoolgirl. At that first interview, I didn't get any sexual vibe from her either. Anyway, she soon let me know she had a boyfriend and it was all as clear and distinct as in Descartes's *Discourse*. My daughter adored her right from the start. She drew her a picture every day. And she rushed to hug her when she arrived in the morning. At least that part is true: Pauli fantasised that they were sisters. Luciana was very good with her. She'd give her one of her hairslides, and stickers from her file. She listened patiently to Pauli's little stories and let her drag her off to her playroom for a while after she'd finished work. But I was the one who benefited the most: after hiring her I got on with my novel better than ever before. I thought I'd found the perfect system. She was intelligent and alert, I never had to repeat a sentence, and she kept up without making mistakes however fast I dictated. True, I never dictated long chunks in one go – I'm not exactly fluent – but now I could pace up and down my study, almost talking to myself, and not have to worry. I also trusted her to point out if there needed to be a comma somewhere or if I'd repeated a word. I was delighted with her work, and I became truly fond of her. At the time, I was working on a novel about a sect of Cainite assassins, and for the first time in my life as a writer I was completing a page a day. And of course, as an unexpected bonus, she was pleasing to look at. I had paced my study for years, alone, eyes on the floor, but now I could look up every so often and be comforted simply by seeing her there, sitting up straight in my chair, ready for the next sentence. Yes, she was very pleasing to look at, but I was too happy with our arrangement to jeopardise it. I was only concerned with getting on with my work so I made sure I didn't get too close to her, or touch her even by mistake. The only physical contact was a kiss on the cheek when she arrived and another when she left.'

'So how did it all happen?'

'Yes, I've often wondered myself about the *progression*. As you can imagine, it wasn't just one thing. At first I simply noticed that she wanted to please me but I didn't give it much thought. It seemed normal: it was her first job and she wanted to do well. A couple of times I almost told her she was doing fine and didn't have to try so hard. I thought I conveyed this in various ways, but perhaps I seemed too serious, or distant. Perhaps she was a little afraid of me. Anyway, she took pains over the slightest detail, and it was almost as if she could read my mind. She often guessed what I wanted her to do even before I asked. This did intrigue me – the way she'd got to know me in such a short time. I mentioned it to her once and she said that maybe it was because I was a little like her father. One day I complained that the Bible I was consulting for my novel wasn't annotated and the following morning she brought that great big Scofield Bible you've seen yourself. That's when I found out that, alongside his day job, her father had a parallel life as a minister in a movement known as dispensationalism. I didn't even know such a group existed. They're fundamentalists: they interpret the Bible literally. Her father was quite high up in the hierarchy: Luciana said he officiated at baptisms. She must have had a very strict religious upbringing, though she never talked about it. I can see from your face that you had no idea.'

'No. I never would have guessed she came from a particularly religious family.'

'She was probably trying to get away from it. Maybe that was one of the reasons she got a job. It was the only time she mentioned her father. She joked about it, as if his religion was something she no longer really believed in – a harmless activity that she was slightly ashamed of. She said her mother didn't really share her father's views. And she herself definitely tried to make sure it didn't show. But something remained – the rather earnest, virtuous look, the need to do everything perfectly. Yes, there was still something churchy about her. Parents leave their mark. Though by the time she started working for me I think she'd already discovered she could kneel down to do more than pray.'

He'd said this last sentence without seeking a look of complicity from me, as if simply stating something he'd worked out himself. This did, I reflected, chime with my first image of Luciana: a determined young woman who'd mastered the basic arts of sexual attraction and was keen to extend her repertoire.

'As I said, at first, that's all it was: small attentions. Little things. She was always solicitous, attentive. But then I realised that Luciana was seeking more than gratitude: she wanted me to *notice her*. She started keeping her hand on my shoulder a little longer when we kissed goodbye, she dressed differently, she sought my gaze more often. I found it amusing and didn't attach much importance to it. I thought it was simply teenage vanity, the arrogance of pretty women who want all men to look at them. At the time I was dictating an erotic section of the book to her. Actually, now that I knew about her background I was worried that she'd run away, terrified. In the novel, the two women seducing the central character had large breasts and I'd described them at some length. I suppose it might have wounded her pride and made her want to prove to herself that in spite of her disadvantage she could nevertheless attract me.

'In the next chapter I mentioned that one of the women had a mark on her arm from a viper's bite – the wound had festered, leaving a deep scar, the size of a small coin. It was early spring and Luciana was wearing a fine long-sleeved T-shirt. She said she had a similar scar from a vaccination, and she pulled the T-shirt off her shoulder to show me. I was standing beside her and saw her bare shoulder, the bra strap she'd moved, the slight dip between her breasts, and her arm, innocently held up for inspection. For a moment, I stood frozen at the sight of the scar: it was deep and round, like a cigarette burn. Above all, I realised she wanted me to *touch* it. I placed my thumb there, and made a gentle circling movement. I think she sensed my agitation. When I looked up and met her eyes I saw the briefest flash of triumph before she hitched up her bra strap and T-shirt again casually. For a time, nothing else happened. That small victory seemed to be enough for her. She'd wanted to attract my attention and she'd succeeded. I realised, reluctantly, that I was now watching her every morning, waiting for another signal or glance. Then, one day, she began this little pantomime with her neck: she'd tilt her head from side to side, making the bones crack, or lean it back every so often, as if she was in pain.'

'Yes, that's right,' I broke in, unable to believe it. 'The thing with her neck. She did it with me too.'

But Kloster didn't seem to hear and went on, absorbed in his account.

'I asked what the matter was, of course, and she gave me an explanation I only half believed, about posture, and tension in the arms and neck when typing. Apparently, anti-inflammatories didn't relieve the pain so she'd been advised to take up yoga and get massages. I asked where exactly it hurt. She leaned forward slightly, sweeping her hair out of the way with her hand. It was a trusting, spontaneous movement. I could see her long bare neck, proffered to me, and the precise outline of the vertebrae. She pointed to a spot somewhere in the middle. I placed my hands on her shoulders and slid my thumbs up and down her neck. She sat rigid, motionless . . . expectant. I think she was as agitated as I was. But she didn't say a word and gradually I felt her give herself up to the movement of my hands. A wave of heat rose into them from her shoulders. I could feel her neck and everything in her yielding, melting beneath the pressure of my fingers. But then I think she suddenly sensed the danger, uneasy at having lost herself for a moment. She sat up, pushed her hair back, and thanked me, as if I'd really helped the pain, saying she felt much better. Her face was flushed but we both pretended it had been something unimportant, not worth mentioning. I asked her to make coffee and she got up without looking at me. When she came back, I went on dictating as if nothing had happened. I'd say that was the second move in the sequence.

'I thought it would all end there, that she wouldn't want to take it any further. But still, every day, I waited for the next move. I was starting to find it hard to concentrate on my novel, always watching for any tiny signal she might give. I had arranged a trip to a writers' retreat in Italy, for a whole month, and now I regretted it. Since I'd started dictating my work to Luciana, I couldn't imagine sitting in front of the computer, working alone again. But of course I couldn't take her with me. I think I was afraid that the growing unspoken closeness between us would be interrupted. She didn't mention her neck again, but the day before I left, she cracked it, as if the pain had never gone away. I slid my hand under her hair and pressed. I asked if it was still painful and she nodded, without looking up. I started massaging the area with one hand and she leaned her head forward slightly as my fingers moved upwards. I placed my other hand on the side of her neck, to support her head. She was wearing a loose blouse, with the top button undone, and when I slid my hands round her neck I shifted the fabric and another button came undone. She didn't do it up. We were both rigid, as if hypnotised, the only movement my hands on her neck. At one point I slid them down to her shoulders and realised she wasn't wearing a bra. I leaned forward slightly and glimpsed the small points of her breasts, like those of a little girl, barely covered by the blouse. For some reason this sudden unexpected nudity made me stop. This time it was I who drew back, feeling I was one step from the abyss. I moved away, while she gathered her hair in her hands, twisting it nervously. Still not looking at me, she asked if I'd like her to make coffee. I suppose this was the decisive moment in the sequence. But I let it pass.

'When she returned from the kitchen she'd done up her blouse, and it was as if nothing had happened between us. We agreed that I'd ring her when I got back from my trip and I paid her for the whole month I'd be away, hoping she wouldn't take another job. We said goodbye as if it was any other day. I bought her a present in Italy, though I never got to give it to her. The month passed and I called her as soon as I got back. I thought it would all be as before and we'd continue where we'd left off, with that subterranean, almost imperceptible, current between us, moving us in only one direction. But something – everything – had changed. When I asked what she'd done while I was away she mentioned you. From her tone of voice, the way her eyes shone, I thought I understood everything.'

'Everything?' I interrupted, unable to stop myself. 'But it was nothing. She only let me kiss her once.'

Now, Kloster looked at me closely. He sipped his coffee, peering at me again over his cup, as if unsure whether he could trust me.

'It didn't seem like that from what she said. Or rather, from what she implied. Of course I couldn't ask her directly, but from something she said the message was clear, and somewhat humiliating. She gave me to understand that you'd moved quickly during that month. Anyway, I couldn't dictate a single line. I was furious, and obsessed with the thought that I'd lost her. She seemed like a stranger, sitting there in her chair, someone I really knew nothing about. I couldn't focus on my work at all. I realised bitterly that using typists and stenographers had worked for Henry James because he was indifferent to the charms of women. The great Disrupter is not Evil – nor the infinite as our Poet believed – but sex. Like my wife, I had underestimated Luciana. And now I was abject, in thrall to her, like a sex-obsessed teenager. I despised myself. I couldn't believe this was happening to me again at my age. Several days passed like this: I grew increasingly tense; I couldn't dictate at all. It was as if the silent barrier she'd erected had also blocked the flow of my novel. I couldn't move forward with her but I was afraid now that I couldn't move forward without her either. What I'd once considered the perfect system had become a nightmare. My most ambitious novel, the work I'd spent years nurturing in silence, to which all my previous novels had been precursors, was now halted, interrupted, as I waited for a vibration, a note, from her motionless, closed-off body.

'At last one morning I managed to pull myself together and recover my momentum, my self-respect. I began dictating one of the most cruel scenes of the novel – the first methodical slaughter by the Cainite assassins – and I found myself being carried along by my words. They seemed to be dictated by another voice inside me, a free, savage, powerful voice. I, who had so often mocked myths of inspiration, the romantic posing of writers who boasted that their characters dictated orders to them. I, who had always written just one sentence at a time, wavering, regretting my choice of words, making minute corrections, was now swept along by a wave of vociferous primitive violence that left no time or room for doubt, that spoke for me in a fierce but welcome outpouring. I dictated at unprecedented speed, the sentences rushing, tumbling out one after another, but Luciana kept up and never interrupted. She seemed to be possessed by the same facility, as if she were a virtuoso pianist only now allowed to show off her skill. It lasted maybe a couple of hours, though it seemed time no longer existed and I was in a trance beyond human measure. I glanced over Luciana's shoulder and saw that we'd advanced by ten pages – more than I usually wrote in a week. I was overcome by good humour and saw her differently for the first time in days. Maybe I'd exaggerated and jumped to conclusions. Maybe she just wanted to wound me, and mentioning you was an adolescent tactic to make me jealous. I made a couple of jokes and she laughed in the same relaxed way as before. In my enthusiasm, my sudden euphoria, I misread the signs. I asked her to make coffee. She straightened in the chair, arched her back, and then rubbed her neck and made that cracking sound I'd waited for for so long. I was standing very close to her and thought it was her way of sending me a sign, of checking that her secret signal still worked. A second chance. I placed my hands on her shoulders and drew her towards me so as to kiss her. I'd made a fatal mistake. She struggled and pushed me away. I let go of her immediately but she screamed, as if she really thought I was going to attack her. We stood for a moment in silence. She was shaking and looked distraught. I couldn't understand what had happened. I hadn't even touched her lips.

'My daughter came to the door. I suddenly realised that my wife might also have heard the scream. I managed to reassure Pauli and when she closed the door

Luciana and I were alone again. She went to pick up her bag and looked at me with horror and disgust, as if I'd committed an unforgivable crime. With barely contained fury she said she'd never set foot in my house again. I found her tone of moral outrage infuriating, but I managed to control myself. I simply said that she'd given me all the signals. This made her even angrier. She kept saying, "What signals? What signals?" getting louder and louder. She stumbled over her words and seemed on the verge of tears. I was completely taken aback – her reaction seemed so sudden and excessive, but in the confusion of accusations I heard her say she'd sue me and slowly it all seemed to acquire a different meaning. A sordid, repellent meaning. I remembered that a few days earlier she'd seen me sign several contracts for translation rights. She could easily have seen the sums involved. And in emails I'd sometimes discussed my earnings. I'd always been particularly generous to her. It was my way of showing I was pleased with her work. She saw me taking trips and accepting invitations from different countries. She must have thought I was a millionaire.'

'She told me that at the time she wasn't really thinking of suing you, it was just an empty threat. It was her mother who persuaded her. Surely you don't believe it was all part of a plan? That she could have been so calculating?'

'I've just read the fairy tale she told you,' he said

113

coldly. 'Don't you find it odd that she left out so much? You can ask her about everything I've just said. Or do you believe that I would jump on a woman out of the blue? Nothing like that had ever happened to me: I couldn't understand it. I don't mean the rejection, but her extreme reaction. The only thing that made sense of it was her threat to sue me. I couldn't believe it at first. After she'd left I wondered endlessly if I had really done something so bad. I'd only tried to kiss her. Once. I dismissed it as an empty threat, but then the solicitor's letter arrived. No doubt about it, two days later there it was. I was alone in my study when I opened it. I saw her handwriting and the absurd sum she was suing me for and still thought it was something she'd done in the heat of the moment after she left that day. The first line, with the accusation of sexual harassment, made me boil with indignation. But it seemed so crazy that I didn't even consider replying. I simply tore it up so that my wife couldn't read it. I'd told Mercedes that Luciana would no longer be coming because she'd got a full-time job. She was surprised Luciana hadn't said goodbye to Pauli but left it at that. Pauli, on the other hand, wouldn't stop asking for her.

'A month passed and nothing more happened so I thought things must have blown over. But then the postman rang the bell again one morning. I was in my study and, not wanting to disturb me, my wife went down to sign for me. By the time she knocked at the door to hand me the letter, she'd read the name of the sender. She placed it on my desk and stood behind me, arms crossed, waiting for me to open it. I think she read the first line at the same time as I did. It was a repeat of the first letter, demanding more money. My wife saw those two words, the despicable accusation, and tore it from my hands. By the time she'd finished reading it, Mercedes was shaking with hatred and joy. It was the opportunity she'd been waiting for for a long time – the chance to leave and take Pauli away from me for ever. She screamed insults, waving the letter, saying she was going to keep it, so that when Pauli grew up she'd know what kind of person her beloved daddy really was. Of course she wouldn't let me explain. She wouldn't listen to anything I said and I don't think I would have had the strength to explain at the time anyway. I'd lied to her the day Luciana left and in her eyes this could only mean I was guilty. I was stunned, reduced to silence. I felt a disastrous sequence of events had been set in motion and all I could do was wait for the consequences. In fact our marriage had been over for a long time. But before I tell you about Mercedes, to be fair to her there's something I must show you,' he said suddenly, and stood up. 'If I can find it. Or better still, come with me.'

I got to my feet, and he indicated an archway leading to another part of the house.

7

I followed him down a wide corridor with an oak floor. There were several doors leading off it, all closed. He opened the end door and we went into his study. The first thing I noticed was the large window looking on to an unexpected sunken garden, with several trees, and climbing plants covering the walls. In the fading light I could see an immense desk covered in books and papers, with two rows of drawers, and a swivel chair in front of it. A laptop occupied a small space in the middle, between piles. A chaotic jumble of yet more papers and books seemed to have accumulated at different times on a table in the centre of the room. Kloster motioned me to the only other chair, miraculously clear, and started searching through desk drawers. At last he seemed to find what he was looking for, pulling from the bottom of a drawer an old, slightly creased TV listings magazine with an actress I didn't recall on the cover.

'This is the only photo of Mercedes I've kept. Here she is, as she was when I met her,' he said, handing me the magazine. I realised it was his way of explaining why he'd married her, of showing me the only, misguided but excusable, reason. Across the years the hairstyle looked slightly ridiculous, but the face and eyes were captivating. The sensual pout still achieved the desired effect, and there was something resolute in the full curves of the body, displayed with studied nonchalance. I thought to myself that it must have been difficult to take your eyes off her. Kloster switched on a lamp and went to the window. He stood with his back to me, looking out at the deepening gloom of the garden, as if he wanted to keep away from the photo.

'Not long after we were married, before Pauli was born, I started noticing the first signs of . . . instability. I suggested we separate but she threatened to kill herself if I left. I believed her. We had a sort of truce and, with desperate cunning, she made sure she got pregnant. She had an appalling pregnancy with a series of complications, but I couldn't tell if they were real or imaginary. After the birth, Mercedes was exhausted and stayed in bed for a month. She rejected the baby. She wouldn't touch her, she wouldn't even let me bring her near her. I had terrible trouble convincing her to hold her long enough to breastfeed. She said Pauli had drained her completely and was now sucking the remaining life out of her. It was shocking to see: she really did seem to have lost something irrevocably during the pregnancy. Her face had become bloated, her features sunk in fat, and she didn't get her figure back. When at last she got out of bed she started eating with cold determination, like an automaton, as if she wanted to do herself as much harm as possible. And, as if it had flown off and alighted intact, all her beauty was superimposed on Pauli's little face. I'd never seen such a close resemblance, apparent so early, in a baby. She looked exactly like her mother, like Mercedes at her most luminously beautiful, when I first met her.

'Mercedes eventually came to accept her, but in the meantime Pauli had got used to me and she cried if Mercedes tried to hold her. This didn't help, of course. I persuaded Mercedes to see a therapist and for a time things seemed to improve. She made an effort to get close to the baby and eventually Pauli stopped crying with her. She also tried to lose weight, but didn't manage it. After a while, she gave up: she'd decided not to go back to work anyway. In fact she was entirely absorbed by one thing only: getting Pauli away from me. I'd taken care of the baby day and night for the first months so of course she was more attached to me. I adored that little girl,

with a violent, absolute love that I'd never felt for anything or anyone. Not for Mercedes, and she knew it. She
couldn't conceal her jealousy and did everything she
could to keep me away from the child. The first word
Pauli said was "Daddy" and Mercedes accused me of
teaching her to say it, secretly, behind her back, just to
humiliate her. In her madness she really believed we were
at war. Things got even worse because Pauli took a long
time to learn to say "Mummy". That's when I noticed
the first symptoms of something that terrified me so
much I couldn't even admit it to myself: Pauli was afraid
of being alone with her mother. I started finding small
marks on her skin: scratches, sometimes a bruise. It only
happened when the two were left alone. But there was
always a reasonable explanation, because in her own
way Mercedes was very clever. Sometimes, before I got a
chance to ask, she'd say that Pauli had had an accident,
or that she'd scratched herself because her little nails
were too long. She pretended to be even more worried
than I was by these small injuries. But I noticed that she
left hot cups of coffee within Pauli's reach, and didn't
rush after her if she started crawling towards the stairs.
She seemed to be looking for ways for Pauli to injure herself. Of course that was too horrible to contemplate, and
I couldn't think how to confront Mercedes. I felt Pauli's
life was in danger and that I could only keep her safe if I
had her in sight at all times. I made sure she learned to

speak as early as possible: I wanted her to be able to tell me if her mother hurt her. And indeed as soon as Pauli could speak she no longer had any accidents or injured herself.

'For a while I thought the nightmare was over, but it was only a temporary reprieve while Mercedes planned her next move. She hated her daughter – there's no other word to describe it. Especially because since Pauli had learned to speak she had made it even more obvious how much she adored me. Mercedes couldn't stand it and, for the first time, *she* mentioned divorce. She'd been against separating but now, coldly, methodically, she started echoing the reasons for it that I'd given her years earlier. But the real reason, and we both knew it, was that she knew she'd get custody of Pauli. It was a perfect, simple way of taking her away from me. I was desperate. I bluffed, I pleaded, I humiliated myself. For the first time she sensed the power her threat gave her. And she made the most of it. It was a new toy, a source of unexpected pleasure. Like the fisherman's wife in *One Thousand and One Nights* she demanded, demanded, demanded. And I gave her whatever she wanted. Mainly it was money – money we couldn't afford. She delighted in squandering it on fripperies in front of me. She became cynical and when she made some particularly large expenditure she said it was for the good of literature, because now I'd have to write another novel. I made myself write a book in under a year, far quicker than usual, just to get the advance. In the novel a writer strangles his wife. I knew she wouldn't even bother to read it. It's exactly what I should have done – strangled her. Because then Pauli would be alive today. But I thought I'd found a way to appease her and that with our monstrous pact Pauli was safe. Mercedes made fun of her and her infatuation with me, but otherwise she left her alone.

'However, I never completely dropped my guard, so when I spent that month in Italy I hired the nurse who'd looked after my mother at the end as a nanny for Pauli. I spoke to her privately; she was the only person to whom I'd ever confided my fears for Pauli's safety. She listened and promised she wouldn't let Pauli out of her sight, and would watch over her even while the child was asleep. She'd once looked after a woman with Munchausen's syndrome by proxy, whose behaviour was very like Mercedes's, and she suggested I seek medical help on my return. I telephoned every day and it all seemed to be going well. Too well. When I got back, I realised that Mercedes had given a perfect performance during that month, convincing the woman that she was a devoted mother and that I was a dangerous deviant who'd been trying to turn Pauli against her since she'd been born. I sensed that the two of them had formed an alliance. I found out later – much later, unfortunately – that the nurse had told Mercedes everything I'd said about her. This must have put her on the alert and precipitated her plans, but I didn't pay enough attention to the signs. I was so happy to be back, to hug Pauli again, and especially to know I'd be seeing Luciana again the following day.'

He paused, and when he spoke again he sounded desolate, as if he still couldn't make sense of the sequence of events.

'Then there was the business with Luciana, and suddenly Mercedes was holding that letter. Her letter of triumph. In less than forty-eight hours she'd initiated divorce proceedings and obtained a court order barring me from the house – the house bought entirely with my money. She stayed on there with Pauli. I had to go to a hotel while my solicitor appealed against the order. I'd never had to go to a lawyer before and now I was involved in two cases. In my first visit to the solicitor's office I learned an unforgettable lesson about what I could expect from the justice system. I started to tell the solicitor what had happened with Luciana but he stopped me: what had taken place between the two of us when we were alone in a closed room would be of no interest to a judge as it was Luciana's word against mine. Legally the accusation of sexual harassment had no importance: it was simply a way of officially stating that she'd been dismissed. "The law doesn't care about the truth," he said, "but only about versions that can be proved." The discussion would shift to the question of unpaid social security contributions and pension payments. In other words, bits of paper that could be produced. I was to be quite clear that it all boiled down to money and I would have to decide whether I wanted to settle by offering such-and-such a sum during the conciliation phase, or wait for the judge to specify a different figure after the court case.

'I pointed out that the line in Luciana's letter about sexual harassment was being used by my wife to support her divorce petition. The solicitor said I should prepare myself for much worse accusations: it was all part of the game. I told him about my fears for Pauli's safety, now that she was alone with her mother. He asked if anyone else had seen the cuts and bruises I'd found on Pauli when she was a baby. He said he had children himself and they often hurt themselves. Perhaps my wife was less vigilant than I was? Had Pauli ever had a particularly serious accident? Did she have any permanent marks or scars? Was I absolutely certain that my accusations were well founded? I had to admit that nothing bad had happened to Pauli in the past few years. He asked if the nurse I hired during my absence had noticed anything unusual that she might testify to. I had to say no. He held up his hands as if to say there was nothing he could do. Again, he said, it would be my word against another's. I asked if we couldn't file a writ, even if only as a warning. He said no judge would take it into consideration, because you needed much more than a vague accusation to deny custody of a child to its mother. He thought it best not to use their ploys, but to play the rationality card throughout the case. He told me to leave both matters with him and that he'd get on with obtaining an access order as soon as possible so that I could see Pauli again.

'It took almost a month, during which time the first conciliation meeting with Luciana took place. The solicitor attended alone as I wanted nothing to do with it. All I cared about was seeing Pauli. At last the order arrived, specifying my visitation schedule. My first day was a Thursday afternoon at five. I telephoned a little before the hour but no one answered. I assumed it was another of Mercedes's tricks to irk me. I went to the house that had once been my home and rang the doorbell, but no one came. I tried my key but Mercedes had had the lock changed. I saw a light at one of the windows and called out my daughter's name. No answer. I thought I was going to lose my mind. I went to get a locksmith and the man managed to force open the door. I rushed upstairs and saw Mercedes's inert body on the bed, a bottle of pills on the bedside table. I didn't stop to go to her. I was calling Pauli's name, but there was a deathly silence in the house. She wasn't in her bedroom or the playroom. Then

I saw the light in the bathroom. I went in and drew the shower curtain. Pauli was there, submerged in the bath, white, motionless, her hair floating around her face like seaweed. She'd drowned in twelve inches of water. She could have been dead for hours. I snatched her out of the water. She was cold and slippery. The clothes she was going to wear on her outing with me lay folded on a chair. From somewhere very far away I heard the locksmith shouting: Mercedes was alive and the man was saying we should call an ambulance.'

'So what had happened? You don't think she . . .'

'According to her statement she started drinking – a couple of glasses of brandy – while she was running Pauli's bath. She left her in the bath and went to lie down for a while. She said she'd had an exhausting day and fell asleep for a little over an hour. When she woke up she couldn't hear any sounds of splashing so she rushed to the bathroom. She found her as I did, drowned in the bath. She didn't try to pull her out. She said she just wanted to kill herself when she saw her like that. She couldn't stand the thought that it was her fault. So she went back to the bedroom and swallowed all the sleeping pills in the bottle. But there weren't that many, at least not enough to kill her. And because Mercedes knew when I'd be arriving for my visit, she could count on me finding her in time. And that's what happened. They pumped her stomach and she was fine.'

'But there must have been an investigation. Or did they accept her story?'

'There was an investigation and they believed her story. In the forensic analysis they found that Pauli had a haematoma on the back of her head. According to their reconstruction of events, Pauli had tried to get out of the bath on her own. She must have slipped and banged her head, losing consciousness before sliding under the water. Maybe she cried out as she fell but if you accepted that Mercedes was asleep, you could also accept that Pauli's cry didn't wake her. The way in which water had filled the lungs was compatible with Pauli's having lost consciousness beforehand.'

'But you accused her?'

Kloster was silent for a moment, as if my question came from a distant dimension, or was in a foreign language. He looked at me as if I belonged to a different species.

'No. When you hold your dead child in your arms, everything changes. And I'd already seen what I could expect from the justice system. But I knew who the real culprit was. And the laws of men would never touch her. During that time I felt as if I weren't part of the human race. Some time before, for my novel on the Cainites, I'd looked at some ideas on the law, even dictating a few notes on it to Luciana. It was a purely intellectual exercise. First I looked at the ancient law of retaliation, the *lex talionis*, which is part of the Code of Hammurabi: a life for a life, an eye for an eye, a tooth for a tooth, a hand for a hand. A law we tend to consider cruel and primitive. But if you look at it another way, it's on a human scale, with an element of equivalence that's merciful: it recognises the other as an equal, and limits retribution. Because in fact the first ratio of punishment in the Bible is the one laid down by God as a warning to anyone who would kill Cain – seven to one. Of course, this might be the proportion that God reserves for himself, in his absolute power. It's always in the interests of the powers that be for punishment to be excessive, unforgettable. Above all, to act as a warning. But also, I wondered, given its source in the highest divinity, the "fount of all justice", could there be something more here than simply the will to crush? Could there even be a kernel of reason in the disproportion? The will, perhaps, to distinguish between attacker and attacked? To ensure that they're not equal when it comes to the harm done and that the aggressor suffers more than the victim? How would one mete out punishment if one were God? I'd made the notes almost as a game, to prepare for my novel. But now my daughter was dead and the words I'd dictated suddenly made no sense. Because any idea of justice, or reparation, looks forward to the notion of a future and a community of men. But I felt that something inside me was broken for ever. That I no longer belonged to any community or any future. That I stood, howling, outside humanity. When I went over the papers, I also came across the Bible Luciana had lent me and I remembered, as if it were part of another life, someone else's life, that I had to attend a conciliation meeting because of the letter that had set everything in motion. I called my solicitor and dispensed with his services: as I told him, I wanted nothing more to do with human justice. I attended the meeting myself and returned the Bible to Luciana. The red bookmark was at that page because that's where I had left it after dictating my notes to her. It wasn't meant as a threat. I just wanted her to *know*. Strange, everything that happened afterwards, that series of . . . of misfortunes, because the punishment I'd imagined for her was in principle very different.'

He fell silent, as if he couldn't continue, or had said something he might regret later.

'But why punish Luciana for your daughter's death? Wasn't your wife to blame?'

'You don't understand. As I said, Mercedes and I had a pact. And until that time we had respected it. Have you ever played Go?' he asked suddenly.

I shook my head.

'Sometimes the game reaches a point at which players are condemned to repeating the same moves indefinitely – the Ko position. Neither player can break the stalemate because if they make any other kind of move they lose the game immediately. That is what my days with Mercedes were like. We'd reached an equilibrium. A Ko position on which Pauli's life depended. It was a question of time, until Pauli was grown. But Luciana's letter destroyed everything.'

'You said that you imagined a punishment for her. What was it?'

'I just wanted her to *remember*. To remember, as I did, every day, first thing in the morning and last thing at night, that though she was alive my daughter was dead. I wanted her life to be stopped, as mine was, at that memory. It's why I went to Villa Gesell that first summer. I knew she'd be there. I couldn't bear the thought of her spending days in the sun while Pauli was for ever buried in the ground, in that little box where I'd had to leave her. I wanted Luciana to see me, day after day. This was my only plan for revenge. I never dreamed her boyfriend would be so stupid as to go for a swim that morning. I saw him disappear, from the promenade as I was leaving, but I just thought he'd swum out too far. I only found out he'd drowned when I went to have coffee as usual the next morning. I must say I was shocked by his death, but for a different reason. I'd always been an atheist, but I couldn't help seeing symmetry, a sign from on high, in the coincidence: my daughter had drowned in the bath and that boy had also drowned, even though he was a lifeguard, as if a finger had pushed him under. And wasn't the sea like a god's bathtub? In an accidental but *magical* way – in the old sense of sympathetic magic – the primitive law of an eye for an eye, a tooth for a tooth had been observed. As she said to you, we now had one death each. But was this enough? Was the balance truly even? Suddenly the question I'd pondered in an abstract way a few months earlier was before me in real life. I decided to return to Buenos Aires to start a novel – the one I mentioned to you. I've been writing it very slowly, with breaks, alongside all the others, for the past ten years. How would one mete out punishment if one were God? We are not gods, but in his own pages every writer is a god. I've devoted myself to writing this secret novel at night. Page by page, it's my way of praying. But that's all I've done, all I've ever really done these past years. I haven't seen Luciana again.'

'But she said she saw you at the cemetery the day of her parents' funeral. Was it a coincidence that you were there that morning?'

'I'm there *every* morning. She'd have seen me any other day: I visit my daughter's grave on my daily walk. And Luciana was the one who saw me. I didn't find out about her parents' death until later, when I received that letter, the letter in which she asked me to forgive her. She begged and pleaded, as if I were behind all her misfortunes. Or had the power to prevent them. From the construction of her sentences, I realised that she was already slightly disturbed. Even so, when her brother was murdered, she managed to get the police to believe her. She wanted to blame his murder on me as well. That policeman, Ramoneda, came to see me. He was very apologetic but said he had to follow up every lead, as the case had acquired great importance because of the scandal of the convicts' being let out to commit robberies. He wanted to know if I'd corresponded with any of the inmates. I explained that, because my novels generally dealt with death and murder, people often thought of them as crime fiction and they were popular with prisoners. I said that over the years I'd received letters from inmates of various prisons, sometimes pointing out mistakes in my books and suggesting their own stories as subjects for future novels. He asked to see the letters so I gave him those I'd kept. He talked about Truman Capote while he was looking at them. He was proud to have read *In Cold Blood* and be discussing it with me. He showed me the rather bizarre anonymous letters. They read like something written by a scorned mistress. He asked if, as a writer, I could infer anything about the author, male or female. I never dreamed he might be setting a trap, or suspected *me* of having written them. Up until that moment I thought he simply wanted to know about my correspondence with inmates of that prison. I told him the little I could tell about the person who'd written the letter and that's when he mentioned Luciana. He'd already made inquiries at her psychiatric clinic and apologised for bringing up something so personal from the distant past. I showed him her letter. He compared the handwriting to that of the anonymous letters. She seemed to be more of a suspect than me. He said he was used to receiving confessions in the most unexpected and strange ways. He mentioned *The Tell-Tale Heart* by Poe. I think he wanted to show me that he too had read a few books. We chatted for a while about crime writers and he looked around my library. I realised he was hoping I'd give him one of my books, so I did and finally he left. It was the last I heard about both the investigation and Luciana, and I assumed that was the end of it. Until I got your call.'

He went to the desk, where I'd left the magazine, and replaced it in the drawer. He lowered the window blind and motioned for me to follow him. We returned to his study in silence. The little stack of papers was still on the table, but I didn't move to pick them up.

'So is there anything else you'd like to ask?'

I had lots more questions but I knew he'd be reluctant to answer any of them. I decided to try anyway.

'She says here that you loathed anything to do with public exposure. I remember myself how you were almost invisible for years. But then suddenly all that changed.'

Kloster nodded, as if he too had found it surprising.

'After Pauli died I thought I was going to lose my mind. And I would have if I'd stayed shut up in this house. Interviews, conferences, invitations, they all forced me to shave, get dressed, go out, remember who I once was; to think and act like a normal person. They were my only link with the world out there, where life went on. I did it all because I knew that as soon as I got back here I'd be alone again with just one thought. They were my outings to normality, my way of keeping sane. I was playing a part, of course, but when you've lost all will to exist, to persist, playing a part can be the only defence against madness.'

He indicated for me to follow him. 'Come with me,' he said. 'There's something else I'd like to show you.'

We made our way to the corridor where I'd seen the first photograph in the gloom. He flicked the switch and the corridor was lit up. The walls were lined with photos of all sizes, hung very close together, like a ghastly collage, showing the daughter's image repeated in a multitude of poses. As we walked down the corridor Kloster said simply: 'I loved taking photos of her. These are the only ones I managed to save.'

He opened a door and we entered a small room. The walls were bare and the only furniture was a chair in one corner and a metal filing cabinet with a small oblong machine on top. When Kloster turned off the light in the corridor I realised it was a projector. The wall facing us was lit up, there was a click and Kloster's daughter appeared, miraculously returned to life. She was crouching in the distance in what looked like a park or garden. She stood up and ran towards the camera, holding a little bunch of flowers. She headed towards us, happy and excited, and as she held out the flowers her childish voice rang out: 'These are for you, Daddy.' Someone stretched out a hand to take the flowers and she ran back into the garden. The writer had somehow arranged it so that the scene was on a loop and the child ran towards and away from us endlessly, with the same bunch of flowers, the words sounding more eerie and sinister every time: *These are for you, Daddy.* I looked round and saw Kloster's face, partially illuminated by the glare from the wall. He stood rigid, rapt as he watched, eyes fixed and stony like those of a dead man, with only a finger moving mechanically to press the button on the projector.

'How old was she here?' I asked. Really I just wanted it to stop, to escape from this crypt.

'Four,' said Kloster. 'It's my last image of her.'

He turned off the projector and switched on the light. We returned to the library and I felt as if I were re-emerging into fresh air.

'I spent the first few months after her death shut up in that room. I also started writing my novel in there. I was afraid of forgetting her.'

Once again we stood facing each other in the middle of the library. He watched me as I put on my coat, gathered up the printed sheets and slipped them back in the folder.

'You haven't told me what you intend to do with this. Or do you still believe her rather than me?'

'From what you've said,' I replied hesitantly, 'Luciana has no reason to fear any further misfortunes. The series of deaths, so close to her, must have been chance, a run of extremely bad luck. But doesn't it strike you as unusual?'

'Not really. If you toss a coin in the air ten times it's quite likely you'll get heads or tails three or four times in a row. Luciana could have got tails several times in succession over the past few years. Misfortunes, like gifts, are not fairly distributed. And chance, in the long term, may be a superior way of meting out punishments. That is what Conrad believed: "It is not Justice the servant of men, but accident, hazard, Fortune – the ally of patient Time – that holds an even and scrupulous balance." But isn't it paradoxical that I should have to remind you that chance exists? Didn't you write a novel called *The Random Men*? Weren't you the fervent defender of Perec's building and Calvino's pack of cards? Weren't you proud to oppose old-fashioned causality in fiction, the stale determinism of action–reaction? And now suddenly you come here in search of the First Cause, of Laplace's demon, of an unambiguous explanation of the kind you so despised. You wrote an entire novel about chance, but you obviously never bothered to toss a coin in the air. You don't know that chance has its forms and runs as well.'

I said nothing for a moment, holding Kloster's contemptuous gaze. So not only had he read my unfortunate article but he'd remembered it word for word. Wasn't he showing me, despite himself, unwittingly, his bitter, vindictive nature? But then I too remembered every word of bad reviews and could have repeated a few verbatim. And if it didn't make me a criminal, how could I use it against Kloster? I felt I had to say something.

'True, I find classical causality in literature boring, but I can distinguish between my literary views and reality. And I expect that if four of my closest relatives died I too would find it alarming and would start looking for other explanations.'

'Can you really? Distinguish between your fiction and reality, I mean. For good or ill, that was what I found hardest when I began my novel. "Fiction competes with life," said Henry James, and it's true. But if fiction *is* life, if fiction creates life, it can also create death. I was a corpse after I buried Pauli. And though a corpse can't aspire to create life, it can still create death.'

'What do you mean? That there are deaths in your novel too?'

'There is nothing but deaths.'

'But aren't you worried that it'll start to seem . . . unbelievable?' I felt silly, and rather contemptible: Kloster's commitment to verisimilitude in his novels was something I myself had made fun of.

'You don't understand. You can't. It's enough that *I* believe it. It's not for publication. It's not intended to convince anyone. Let's just say it's a personal declaration of faith.'

'But in your novel,' I insisted, 'do you uphold the hypothesis of chance?'

'No, I don't. What I'm saying is that *you* should. Or at least consider it. But I suppose there could be other explanations, for a writer with enough imagination. Even a policeman like Ramoneda was able to conceive of another possibility.'

'Please! The only thing an Argentinian policeman can come up with is that the victim is also the prime suspect. Why would Luciana do such a thing?'

'For the most obvious reason: guilt. She knows she's guilty and she's giving herself the punishment she thinks she deserves. Because her father, a religious fanatic, instilled in her a belief in the whip, in self-flagellation. Because she's crazy, yes, but to an extent that neither you nor I can imagine.'

Kloster said it without emphasis, with the calm coldness of a chess player watching a game, analysing possible moves. I said nothing. Again he pointed at the plastic folder under my arm.

'So what are you going to do with that? You still haven't told me.'

'I'll keep it in a drawer for now,' I said, 'and I'll wait: as long as there are no more tails in the sequence that's where they'll stay.'

'That's rather unfair,' said Kloster, as if trying to talk round a difficult child. 'Unless I'm much mistaken, Luciana's grandmother was already very elderly ten years ago. She was in a care home. And if she hasn't died yet, it could happen at any time.'

I didn't detect any hint of a threat either in his expression or in his voice. He simply seemed to be making a logical objection.

'A death from *natural* causes obviously wouldn't count,' I said.

'But don't you see? Luciana wouldn't consider anything a natural death. Even if her grandmother died in her sleep she'd claim I climbed down the chimney and smothered her with a pillow. She thinks I poison cups of coffee and spread toxic fungi and free prison inmates, so nothing will stop her.'

'But I can judge for myself and I know the difference between a sequence of four tails and one of seven.'

'The number seven,' said Kloster, as if he were suddenly fed up. 'You shouldn't make the same mistake.

Apparently Luciana's father didn't teach her about biblical symbolism. The Hebrew root of the word "seven" is related to the completeness and perfection of cycles. That's the way the number seven is used in the Old Testament. When God warns those who want to kill Cain, he's not referring to a literal number, to a numerical ratio, but to vengeance that is complete and perfect.'

'Don't you think the death of four loved ones is sufficiently complete vengeance?'

Kloster looked at me as if we were arm wrestling and he acknowledged my effort but wasn't prepared to give an inch.

'*I can only know my own pain,*' he said. 'Isn't that, basically, the problem with punishment? A dilemma, as Wittgenstein would say, of private language. I don't know how many deaths are equivalent to the death of a daughter. And anyway it's not something that depends on me, or something I can stop. As I said, I'm simply writing a novel. But I see I haven't convinced you, and it's getting late. I've got an appointment: a girl from a secondary school is coming to interview me for her school paper . . .'

Kloster stopped, possibly because he'd seen the look of surprise and alarm on my face. I hadn't mentioned Luciana's fears for her sister in the pages I'd given him to read. I stood, frozen, waiting for him to say more. But he simply motioned peremptorily towards the stairs, indicating that I should leave at last. As I descended the stairs I turned: he was still standing at the top, as if he wanted to make sure I really was going.

'You said on the phone that you had a question for me,' I remembered suddenly. 'But you haven't asked me anything.'

Kloster made a gesture, almost like a wave.

'Don't worry. You've already told me what I wanted to know.'

8

In the street I looked for a phone. I didn't have my address book with me so I called Directory Enquiries and gave Luciana's name and address. A moment later an automated voice gave me the number. I dialled it immediately before I forgot it.

'I've just spoken to Kloster,' I said. 'He made me leave because a girl was arriving to interview him for her school paper. Could it be your sister?'

For a moment there was silence at the other end.

'Yes, my God, yes,' she said faintly. 'I thought she'd given up on the idea. But she must have arranged it behind my back. She's just gone out. She wouldn't tell me where she was going but I saw her put one of Kloster's novels in her bag. I thought that was odd because she's already read it. She's probably taken it for him to sign.' There was desperation in her voice. 'I could get a taxi, but it's too late now: I don't think I can catch up with her. Where are you calling from?'

'I'm just round the corner from his house, in a call box.'

'Then you could wait for her and stop her, until I can get there. Would you do that for me? I'll get a taxi straight away.'

'No, I'm not going to do it,' I said as firmly as I could. 'You and I need to talk. I'm sure Kloster wouldn't try anything stupid in his own house. There's a café on the corner; I think I can see the entrance to the house from there. I'll keep an eye out until you arrive and then we can talk. I'll sit in the window and wait for you.'

'All right,' she said reluctantly. 'I'm leaving now. I just hope Kloster hasn't convinced you too.'

I went into the café, which was almost empty at that hour, and sat at a table by the window from where I could see Kloster's house across the street. Before I'd even had time to order coffee a small handbag passed the window. I would have recognised it anywhere. I leaned forward to look out but the girl had already crossed the road and a bus at the traffic lights was blocking my view. By the time it moved away there was no sign of Luciana's sister and Kloster's front door was just closing. All I'd glimpsed of her was the handbag inherited from Luciana, and the sleeve of her navy blue coat.

Luciana arrived half an hour later. As she came through the swing doors she glanced at her reflection and made a furtive, desperate attempt to tidy her hair. I realised my call must have got her out of bed and she'd only just noticed what she looked like. Her face was drawn, without make-up, and her eyes were glassy as if she'd taken sleeping pills.

'Has she gone in?' she asked without preamble.

I stood up and gave her my seat so that she could watch the entrance herself, and sat down opposite her.

'Yes, a while ago. Actually I only caught a brief glimpse but I think it was her: she was carrying the handbag you used to have and wearing a navy blue coat.'

Luciana nodded. 'Yes, a long coat. It used to be mine too. What time did she go in?'

'About ten minutes ago. But I told you, nothing's going to happen to her. I spoke to him as you asked.'

'And he convinced you,' she said, looking into my eyes, unrelentingly searching for the truth. 'Now you believe him.'

'I didn't say that,' I said, uncomfortable. 'But I'm sure he wouldn't do anything so *direct*. And certainly not in his own house.'

'He could do other things to her,' she said darkly. 'Valentina has no idea, she's just an impulsive teenager.

She doesn't know what he's like. I don't know what image of him she's built up from his novels. But remember, I know him. I know how captivating he can be.'

'That's really what I wanted to talk to you about. His version of events is pretty different from yours.' I saw her draw back warily.

'I suppose a writer can invent all sorts of stories. What did he say?'

'That when you started working for him it never entered his head to try anything. He was too happy with the arrangement and with the way his work was progressing to ruin it all by trying anything more. He thought you were pretty but he wasn't attracted to you. He said it was you who made him notice you. He told me that on one occasion he was dictating a section about a scar on a woman's arm. He said you showed him the vaccination mark on your shoulder and invited him to touch it.'

'I showed him the mark, that's true, but I never asked him to *touch* it. I didn't think there was anything wrong in it. I'd forgotten all about it. I can't believe he's trying to give it another meaning.'

'He said it was the first time he'd touched you, and you seemed proud to have got his attention. He also said that later on you let him massage your neck.'

'Well, I see you've become good friends. How did you get him to tell you about that? One day he enquired about my neck. I bent my head to show him where it hurt and he started massaging it. It's true that I didn't stop him, but I didn't think he had any other intention. I trusted him. I told you, I thought of him as a father. I didn't think he had anything else on his mind. And it was only one time.'

'One time, and then another. He said he stopped the second time because you weren't wearing a bra.'

'It may well have been twice. And I didn't wear a bra very often in those days.'

'You did when you worked for me,' I said.

'Because I knew I had to be careful around you. But it never occurred to me he was getting ideas. Until he got back from his trip, when he seemed to have turned into a completely different person, none of it had ever occurred to me. But what are you driving at? Even if I did lead him on, which I didn't, even if I was wrong to sue him, does that justify what happened later? Does that justify killing my whole family?'

'Of course not,' I said. 'It doesn't justify anyone's death. I just want to know whether so far, in this part of the story, he was telling me the truth.'

'That all happened,' she said, looking away, 'but he got the wrong idea. And I've told you a thousand times I regret suing him. But I can't believe that this is my punishment.'

'He does blame you for his daughter's death. You were right about that.'

I recounted what Kloster had revealed about his relationship with his wife, the fears he'd had since Pauli's birth, and the unspoken pact he and Mercedes had had in the last few years. Luciana looked increasingly shocked: she seemed to have no idea of any of it. I told her about the wife's reaction, her outburst when she read the accusation at the head of the letter, her immediate decision to get a divorce and the court order she'd used to separate Kloster from his daughter, using Luciana's accusation as justification. I told her how Kloster had had to move out to a hotel, about his waiting to be allowed to see his daughter again, and what happened on the day of his visit. I tried to use the same words as Kloster had when describing that afternoon, from the time when he telephoned to when he found his daughter's body in the bath. I told her about the crypt, the gallery of photos and the film of his daughter holding the little bunch of flowers. By the time I finished, Luciana's eyes were filled with tears.

'But none of it was my fault,' she whimpered.

'Of course not,' I said, 'but he thinks it was.'

'But it was his wife who . . . who . . . It was his wife,' she said helplessly.

'He believes it was your letter that broke their pact. He was sure he could have maintained their agreement for a few more years, until Pauli was older. He put it like this: his daughter would still be alive if his wife hadn't read that letter. And there's something else you're right about: his being in Villa Gesell that summer wasn't a coincidence. He said he couldn't bear the thought that you were carrying on with your life as if nothing had happened, when his daughter was dead. He wanted to be there to make you remember. So that you'd think of her every day, as he did. So that your life should stop, as his had.'

'If that was his only aim, he succeeded a long time ago. But you see he admitted he wanted to get his revenge. That's what I wanted to know. Because I don't expect he confessed to the murders, did he?'

'No. All he said was that as he was leaving the beach that day, from the promenade, he saw your boyfriend disappear from sight out at sea. And when he found out next day that he'd drowned, he felt that, with that death, the law of an eye for an eye and a tooth for a tooth had been carried out. He said it gave him the idea for a novel about justice and proportionate punishment.'

'It wasn't enough for him. My God, Ramiro's death wasn't enough.'

She looked once more across the street while feeling in her pocket for a handkerchief. She glanced at her watch again and dried her eyes.

'Maybe not,' I admitted. 'But he claims that since that day all he's done about it is write his novel. A novel in which you and he are characters. He assured me he hasn't seen you since then and that he only found out your parents had died when he got your letter.'

She shook her head, still looking out of the window. 'That's a lie: he was at the cemetery the day of their funeral.'

'I asked him about that: he goes there every day to visit his daughter's grave. He claims not to have seen you.'

She turned to look at me angrily. 'I suppose I shouldn't have expected him to admit anything. And he seems to have a lie ready for everything.'

'Actually what I found most disconcerting was that he seemed to be telling the truth. He talked as if he had nothing to hide. He even told me something he could have kept secret, about your brother's death, something we didn't know: he did correspond with inmates of that prison at various times. He said the police had looked into it and that he gave Superintendent Ramoneda any letters he'd kept.'

'But there might have been other letters that he got rid of – that he made sure to get rid of,' Luciana interrupted. 'He could have found out from other inmates that that prisoner got out to commit robberies. And if he'd followed my brother and knew he was involved with that woman, all he had to do was send the anonymous letters to goad the killer on. Kloster wrote them. I knew it as soon as I saw them. He can't fool me.'

'He said he and Ramoneda talked about crime fiction

and that at one point the superintendent showed him the anonymous letters and asked him what kind of person he thought could have written them. Apparently the superintendent thought it was more likely it was you.'

She sat in silence for a moment, her hands trembling helplessly.

'Don't you see?' she murmured. 'Don't you see how he twists everything and turns everyone against me? I suppose he tried to make you believe it was me?'

'Actually, no, he didn't. That's what I found most surprising. He seems to think there's another possibility. I suppose it's what he's writing about in his novel. He said I'd never believe it.'

'There is no other explanation: it's him. I don't understand how you can still doubt it. He'll go on and on, until I'm all alone. Until I'm the last one left. That's the revenge he's after. The one he marked in the Bible: seven for one. And now Valentina is in there at this moment. In there with him. I'll never forgive myself if something happens to her. I don't think I can wait any longer,' she said, making as if to stand. I stopped her.

'When I mentioned that section in the Bible he said it was wrong to interpret it that way. That the number seven is actually a symbol of completeness, of the perfectly finished. The vengeance that God reserves for himself. Even if it is Kloster behind the deaths, maybe the punishment is complete.'

'In the novel about that sect that he was dictating to me, the number seven wasn't symbolic. They killed seven members of a family one by one. That's what he's been planning for me from the beginning and that's why he never had that novel published, so as not to give himself away. Did you ask why he was standing outside my grandmother's nursing home?'

I shook my head. 'I couldn't very well subject him to an interrogation,' I said, a little irritably. 'I just tried to get him to talk. And I think I did pretty well.'

Something in my voice made her back down, as if she realised for the first time that she'd asked too much of me.

'I'm sorry. You're right,' she said. 'How did you get him to see you?'

'I said I was writing a novel about the strange series of deaths around you, and I wanted to hear his version of events. I thought it was also a way of letting him know that somebody else is aware of what's happening to you.'

I realised Luciana was no longer listening to me. She was watching Kloster's front door.

'Thank God,' she murmured. 'I can see her. She's just come out of the house.'

I looked round out of the window, but I'd missed Valentina for the second time. She must have been walking away in the opposite direction, because from her seat Luciana could still see her.

'I think she's heading for the subway,' she said.

'Safe and sound, I hope,' I said. 'We can leave now too.' I signalled to the waiter for the bill.

'I'm going to tell her everything tonight. She has to know what he's like, before it's too late. Can I call over the next few days if I notice she's behaving strangely? I feel she's slipping away from me, and I can't watch over her any more.'

'I'm going to Salinas tomorrow,' I said. 'To give a seminar. I'll be away for a fortnight.'

She was silent for a moment, as if I'd said something unexpected and brutal. She looked at me, all her defences down, and I saw the dismay in her eyes, and the abyss of madness dangerously close. Convulsively, almost invol- untarily, she grasped my hands across the table. She didn't seem to realise how hard she was gripping, or that she was digging her nails into my palms.

'Please, don't leave me alone with this,' she said hoarsely. 'I've had nightmares every night since I saw him outside the nursing home. I know something very bad is about to happen to us.'

Gently I freed myself from her hands and stood up. I wanted to get away from there as soon as I could.

'Nothing else is going to happen,' I said. 'Now he knows that somebody else knows.'

9

As I left the café, I thought I was escaping, but outside, far from feeling free, I could still hear Luciana's voice in my mind, begging me not to leave her alone, and feel her hands gripping my wrists. It was a cold night, at the start of a dark, dismal August, but I decided to go for a walk before heading home. Above all I wanted to *think*. Over and over I told myself I'd already done enough for Luciana and shouldn't let myself be swept along by her madness. I wandered through emptying streets, the shops closed and rubbish strewn over the pavements. Now and then I passed *cartoneros*, silent, eyes lowered, hauling their handcarts to the railway station. The tide had ebbed from the city. All that remained was the rotten smell from torn rubbish bags and the sudden, occasional light from an empty bus as it rumbled by.

Did I really believe, as Luciana had accused, that Kloster was innocent? Episode by episode, I had believed that what he'd told me was true. But he had also appeared to be a player who was entirely in control, who could lie with the truth. What he'd told me might have been the truth, but it probably wasn't the entire truth. And also, coldly considering the facts, all explanations (as Luciana had almost screamed at me) seemed to point to Kloster. Because if it wasn't him, what else was there? A series of fantastic coincidences? Kloster had mentioned runs of bad luck. He'd made me feel small – I could still hear his contempt as he mocked me for having written a novel about chance without knowing that such things occurred. I came to a wide avenue and saw a bar frequented by taxi drivers that was still open. I went in and ordered coffee and toast. What exactly had Kloster said? That I should think of tossing a coin. A sequence of three heads or three tails in a row was not unusual. Chance too had tendencies. I found a quarter in my pocket, searched for my pen and spread a paper napkin on the table. I tossed the coin in the air ten times and wrote down the series of heads and tails using dashes and crosses. I tossed the coin another ten times and wrote out a second sequence beneath the first. I went on tossing the coin, with an increasingly deft movement of the thumb, and noted a few more series on the same napkin, one under the other, until the waiter brought my coffee and toast.

As I ate, I looked over the series, marked on the napkin like some strange code. What Kloster had said was true – amazingly true: there were sequences of three or more heads or tails in almost every line. I spread another napkin on the table and, seized by an impulse, I flipped the coin again, aiming to toss it a hundred times, noting the results tightly so that the entire sequence fitted on the one napkin. The coin slipped from my fingers a couple of times and the clatter made the waiter look round. The bar was empty now and I knew I ought to leave but the repetitive action seemed to have possessed my hand and I couldn't stop. I wrote down the final symbol and looked over the sequence from the beginning, underlining any runs of the same sign. There were series of five, six, even seven of the same sign in a row. So was there, as Kloster had said mockingly, a bias to chance? Even the blind coin yearned for repetition, form, figure. As I tossed the coin more and more times the runs of repetitions grew longer. Perhaps there was even a statistical law that governed their length. And in that case were there other hidden forms, other kernels of causality, within chance? Other figures, other patterns invisible to me, in the sequence I'd just written down? Something that could even explain Luciana's bad luck? I looked at the sequence again but it was still closed to me like some indecipherable handwriting. *You* should uphold the thesis of chance, Kloster had said. I felt something inside me falter, as if an essential, personal foundation, of which I hadn't even been aware, was crumbling. I had withstood the criticism, in a review, that my novel *The Random Men* was calculating in its careful simulation of chance. But simply tossing a coin in the air had proved more devastating than any of these objections. A throw of the dice will never abolish chance, Mallarmé might have said. And yet the napkin spread on the table had demolished for ever what I believed about chance. If you *really* believe in chance, you should believe in these runs, they should seem natural, you should accept them. This was what Kloster had meant, and it was only now that I fully understood. But at the same time – and this was perhaps the most disconcerting thing, the maddening detail – he, Kloster, didn't seem to believe that Luciana's getting tails several times in a row was just a run of bad luck. It was the theory that most favoured and suited him, yet he was sufficiently sure of his innocence, or impunity, to lean towards another possibility. But which one? Of this he had said nothing, merely hinting that it would be set out in his novel. But he had made that strange comparison of the sea to a god's bath. Kloster, the fervent atheist whom I had admired, had spoken in almost religious terms more than once during our conversation. Could his daughter's death have affected him that much? He who stops believing in chance starts to believe in God, I recalled. Was this how it was? Kloster now believed in God? Or had it all been carefully staged to convince a single spectator?

I called the waiter, paid my bill and left. It was past midnight and all you could see in the streets were beggars huddling on bits of cardboard, and foul-smelling piles of black rubbish bags. Now and then refuse lorries ground their metal jaws. I turned down a side street, and was irresistibly drawn to the sudden glow from a shop window. I moved closer and stopped. It was a large furniture store and inside, before my eyes, soundlessly, unbelievably, a fire was spreading. The rug at the entrance was already in flames, slowly writhing and undulating and seeming to rise from the floor. It was smoking and giving off sparks that quickly spread the fire to a coat stand and a coffee table by the door, the flames rising higher and higher. The coat stand suddenly collapsed in a shower of fire, touching the headboard of a double bed. Only then did I notice that the display was arranged as the ideal marital bedroom, complete with bedside tables and a baby's cot. Suddenly the bedcover burst into savage flames. It all happened in the same dauntless silence, the roar of the fire sealed behind the window. I knew the glass might shatter at any moment, but couldn't tear myself away from the hypnotic, dazzling spectacle. Everything writhed before me but still no alarm sounded, no one came, as if the fire was a message for me alone. The room, the cot, the little fake home – it was all disintegrating, transmuting. The furniture was now simply wood, an elemental material seeking only to submit, obey, feed the flames. The fire reared up, a single violent being, malevolent, gleaming, like a dragon twisting and changing form. Suddenly I heard the hysterical wail of a fire engine siren. I realised it was all about to end and tried to hold on to that final indecipherable, breathtaking image behind the glass. Attracted by the siren, the starving creatures of the night, staggering drunks and children who slept in subway entrances, now surrounded me. Above, windows were opening. Then came human voices, orders, a fierce jet of water, and the flames receded, leaving blackened walls. I walked away, not wanting to witness this other, much more depressing spectacle of the fire defeated.

It was very late when I got home. I still hadn't packed for my trip but the flight to Salinas wasn't till after midday so I decided to leave it for the morning. My sleep was heavy with confused images, layer upon layer in quick succession. Still asleep, on the edge of morning, I felt as if I was about to understand something: I simply had to read a succession of dashes and crosses. But I opened my eyes too soon, with that sense of both immi- nence and loss that accompanies images slipping away as you wake. It was nine o'clock. I started packing, and suddenly remembered the fire. I went down to have breakfast in a bar so as to read the paper, and searched for news of the fire. I didn't expect to find anything as it was, all in all, a pretty minor matter and probably wouldn't merit even a short article. But there it was on one of the inside pages, beneath the heading 'As we went to press'. It was a very short item, headed 'Fires'. First it mentioned another fire that had almost entirely destroyed another furniture store. It went on to say that there had been 'two more very similar incidents', in furniture stores in different parts of town. One of them was the fire I had seen, but the article simply gave the location with no other details. The item mentioned that an initial investigation was being carried out to establish whether the fires had been started deliberately. And that was all: no conjectures, just a vague promise that the police were exploring several different avenues.

I folded the paper on the table and ordered another coffee. Three fires in three furniture stores in a single night. Beyond runs of heads or tails, this couldn't be a coincidence. Something stirred in the depths of my memory, trying to rise to the surface. A face came back to me, vehement, mocking, firing out sentences and theories that only held up for a moment, like bubbles in the air, at a café table in the Calle Corrientes, behind the haughty smoke of his cigarette. I could see him again, with his beard and ponytail, surrounded by awed young faces, including my own.

Students, aspiring intellectuals and writers, we all fought to sit near him, listening as he hurled quotations at us and demolished or elevated books with a single sentence – a strange talking machine, malevolent and sarcastic, who also, every so often, had sudden enduring flashes of insight. It was him I thought of first, rather than an arsonist in the most obvious sense. I seemed to hear him again: had it been in our usual bar or at the party to celebrate the only issue of the magazine? Someone had spoken of ephemeral art and street happenings: the stream of paint and Greco's chalk circle around passersby. Someone else mentioned subversive sculpture: the brick flung at the critic's head. Then he had suggested setting fire to furniture stores. Weren't they replicas of the perfect little bourgeois home? The marital bed, the baby's cot, the big round table for family meals, the bookcases to be filled with and display the old culture. The reassuring coffee table in the living room. It was all there, he said, eyes shining mischievously, defiantly. If we wanted to be truly incendiary, there were all the furniture stores of Buenos Aires, waiting for the first match. It would be irresistible. Contagious. A city up in flames, in a single night. Fire, the ultimate, supreme artistic statement, the form to consume all forms.

But could it be him, so many years later? I knew it couldn't: I'd bumped into him again in the street one day and been surprised to find him in a suit and tie. With barely concealed satisfaction, he said he worked for the Ministry of Culture. I had exaggerated my disbelief: he *worked* now? For the *government*? He smiled a little uncomfortably but then tried to return to the ways of the past. That was just it, he defended himself, it wasn't work. It was almost a pension, given to him by the long-suffering taxpayers, the wonderful Peronist people of Argentina. After all, he was only following Duchamp's dictum that the artist should make use of anything – inheritances, grants, private patronage ('And why not the Ministry of Culture?' he said with a wry look) – so as not to have to live by the sweat of his brow.

No, it couldn't be him. But then another thing I'd heard him say in that distant past now came back to me: you shouldn't write about what has been, but about what might have been. For the first time in years I felt I had a *subject*. There had been something providential about the fire of the night before, and the small item in the paper, the modest mystery of the furniture stores, was speaking to me secretly. I left the bar and, a little euphoric, went into a stationery shop and bought a thick hardcover note-book to take with me on the trip. After all, I'd have the mornings free in Salinas so I'd be able to do some writing: maybe I could get a new novel going. I went up to the flat to collect my bag. As soon as I opened the door I saw the red light on the answering machine blinking menacingly, as if it were a remotely activated weapon that could still hurt me. I pressed the button and heard Luciana's voice. She sounded bewildered, desperate, her speech halting, as if she were having trouble threading sentences together. She'd spoken to her sister the night before and told her everything, but she'd sensed that Valentina didn't – wouldn't – believe her. She asked me, begged me, if I hadn't yet left, to ring her. I looked at the clock and picked up my bag. I decided that her call had arrived too late, and I'd already set off for the airport.

10

As the plane soared over the river, reducing the city to a model, I felt, with the sudden lightness of flying, a weight lifting from me. Luciana's story, the conversation with Kloster, even the fire, all appeared small and harmless now too, fading, disappearing into the distance as I left the city behind. I thought of Victorian novels in which the hero or heroine who has fallen in love inappropriately is sent abroad by the parents, a journey that never produces the desired result, only serving to test the strength of love across time and distance. But in my case I had to admit that something was subsiding, as if I really had *escaped*. When, an hour later, I caught sight for the first time of the small town, rising miraculously out of white desert, the buildings set out like dominoes on the cracked, dazzling expanse of salt flats, I genuinely felt I was a thousand miles away.

I submitted to the pleasant welcoming ritual. The dean and one of the professors from the literature department came to meet me at the airport. For my benefit, they took the scenic route back, along the Gran Salina. As we got into town, which looked like an abandoned film set with all the shops closed and streets deserted, they warned me that the siesta lasted until five. They dropped me off at the hotel and came back to collect me a couple of hours later to take me to my first class.

It was meant to be a series of postgraduate seminars, with me giving my usual course on avant-garde literature, but they probably hadn't been able to recruit enough postgrad students so there were some undergraduates as well, there simply to listen. Amongst them, in the second row, I noticed a girl with large, earnest eyes, whom I couldn't help staring at slightly longer than I should. It was a long time since I'd given a class to a whole roomful of students, but thankfully as soon as I picked up the chalk I was transformed: the words flowed and the eloquence I had thought lost for ever returned like a dog that still knew its master. As I reeled off statements, refutations, examples, I felt almost breathless with the euphoria of teaching. Certain theologians maintain that the act of praying can in itself lead to faith, like a quiet, mechanical reaction. In my case the familiar little rituals, the chalk on the board, the opening remarks and, I don't deny it, the student's interested attention, worked their magic once more, the lecture I'd given so many times before coming back to life and the old jokes getting a laugh. But halfway through the exposition, my happy self-confidence faltered and I hung for a moment over the abyss. I was explaining how John Cage had used the hexagrams of the I Ching when composing his piece *Music of Changes*. I'd drawn the figures of six stacked lines representing the notes, with their intensity and duration, and I was about to go over how the hexagrams were cast: by tossing the coins so that the six lines were determined by chance. But as I said the word 'chance', it was as if I had broken a seal and the sequence of heads and tails, the napkin covered in signs proving that chance too followed patterns, slid insidiously back into my mind. What is a loss of certainty like for a lifelong sceptic? It leaves you reeling and unable even to make the most trivial statement. From then on, until the end of the class, something strange and terrifying began to happen: every time I spoke, I felt that a mocking voice inside me was about to add 'or not' at the end of the sentence. Every time I explained something, the little voice wanted to burst out with 'or quite the opposite'. If I was about to state some conclusion (and I made strenuous efforts to make my conclusions appear to stem from faultless reasoning) the voice wanted to jump in and add 'but the opposite is equally valid'. Something had gone awry and signs of this inner conflict must have been apparent to my audience. My confidence evaporated, my pauses grew longer. My voice was faltering horribly and my palms were sweating. I glanced at my watch and saw with relief that I could bring the session to a close. I'd been on the brink of disaster, but hoped my audience would put it down to tiredness. Above all, I wondered what my student with the big eyes had thought. Absurdly, from the very start, I referred to her inwardly as 'my student', as if she were a gift, part of the welcome. I feared she might not be at the dinner that evening for academic staff, but fortunately she was in charge of some formalities relating to my stay, so while I was sign-ing some papers for her we exchanged a few words and I persuaded her to attend. At the table, however, I wasn't seated near her so had to make do with looking at her from afar during the meal.

I woke early the next morning and, heartened by the hotel breakfast, the sunlight streaming through the window and the sight of my brand new notebook, I decided to make a start on my novel about incendiary artists. Two hours later my optimism had disappeared and I decided to go for a walk around the town. I looked round the two or three department stores, entered and quickly left a depressing bookshop, wandered up and down the streets in the centre, and by lunchtime felt as if

I knew the whole place and had exhausted all its possibilities in one walk. I took another walk during the siesta and, paradoxically, at that dead hour, with the streets empty, I found the town more interesting. I pictured thousands of people all horizontal, lying on their beds at the same time, but surely there must be exceptions. Where, I wondered, were the people who resisted the commandment to take a siesta? Crossing the main square and turning down a side street, I saw a neon sign, lit up in full daylight, and steps up to what must have once been a cinema. On a whim, I went through the swing doors to look inside: it was a huge gaming hall. There they were: people of all ages, but mainly middle-aged women, sat hypnotised, silent, on high chairs, mechanically feeding coins into slot machines. There were far more people than I would have expected and I wouldn't have been surprised to find the dean or one of the students there. I came back out on to the quiet streets and walked on. I saw another two or three similar halls, and they were all full of the faithful, as if during the siesta the whole town was engrossed in a Babylon lottery.

That evening I had dinner alone after the class and decided to take a last stroll. There were only a couple of bars open after eleven. In the window of one of them, near the hotel, two prostitutes who were too old and shiny smiled as I passed. By the third night, as I turned

out the light in the now familiar room, I had the feeling
I was trapped inside a video game and already knew all
the locations for the coming levels: the small desk in my
hotel room with the still-empty notebook lying open on
it, the couple of department stores, the dispiriting bookshop, the gaming halls that were strangely full at siesta
time, the solitary cinema, the seminar room at the university, the two bars open late at night. As hero, the
missions I had before me were: possibly writing the first
chapter of my novel; striking it lucky at the slot
machines; sleeping with my student. The dangers that lay
ahead: finding I was addicted to gambling; contracting
an embarrassing disease if I took up the prostitutes'
offer; a minor scandal at the university if I was indiscreet
with my student.

Over the next few days the impulse with which I'd
deluded myself when buying the notebook gradually
wore off. Even the memory of the fire was no longer so
vivid or troubling. At this remove, it seemed almost silly,
its only consequence a few bits of burnt furniture. I followed the news in the Buenos Aires papers from the
computer in the hotel lobby, but the arsonist seemed to
be taking a break as well. I did make an effort with my
student, but by the end of the week I'd given up on this
too. I realised I was almost the same age as Kloster had
been ten years ago, and that there was much the same
age gap between me and this girl as there had been

between him and Luciana. I wondered bitterly if my student had thought, or said to her friends in the same shocked tone as Luciana, that I was old enough to be her father. Still, I had the unexpectedly good idea of putting up a sign outside my small office at the university noting the times when students could consult me. She was the only one who came, bravely alone. And you could say that my luck changed – literally – overnight. Afterwards, she told me she'd decided to make a move because she'd realised that time was running out, as I would only be there another week. As on other trips, I reflected that nothing serves the outsider as well as having a fixed departure date. Of my second week in Salinas I remember only her naked body, her face, her captivating eyes. And though I had already put the entire breadth of the country between Luciana's story and me, I felt even further away from it that week, in that utterly remote world, at the blind, selfish distance that separates the happy from the unhappy.

In fact, I thought of Luciana only once more during that time. One afternoon, J (whom I still call 'my student') was standing in front of the mirror after a shower. As she bent her head and swept her hair to one side to comb it, the sight of her long, bare neck reminded me suddenly of Luciana, as if by a mysterious act of compassion time had restored a fragment of the past to me, luminous and intact. I'd had these impossible encounters before, walking around Buenos Aires, or on trips away, in all sorts of places: faces from the past seeming to appear suddenly, as if to test me, at the age they once were but could no longer be. I'd dismissed it as one more consequence of getting older: the entire human race had started to look strangely *familiar*. But this time the impression was much more vivid, as if Luciana's neck, the neck I'd stared at so amorously day after day, really did exist once more, smooth and vibrant, flesh and bone, part of another's body. I stretched out a trembling, tentative hand and touched the back of her head. J turned for me to kiss her and the illusion vanished.

Two days later it was all over. I gave the students their final grades, packed my bag, including the still-blank notebook, and let J drive me to the airport. We made the usual promises, which we knew we wouldn't keep. My return flight to Buenos Aires was delayed for almost three hours and by the time we took off it was very late at night. I slept for most of the journey, my head resting against the window, but just before landing, as the plane was beginning its descent over the city, I was woken by excited voices around me. The other passengers were looking out, pointing to something down below. I raised the blind and saw, amidst the city lights and rivers of traffic, what looked like the embers of two cigarettes, glowing red points at the base of columns of white smoke. They must have been dozens of blocks apart but from the plane they appeared to be almost side by side. I couldn't quite believe it but it couldn't be anything else: two fires at the same time. The novel I hadn't had the energy to start during my trip seemed to be writing itself down there.

11

I opened the door to my apartment and picked up the bills that lay on the mat. There were no messages on the answering machine, not even from Luciana. Had she left me in peace at last? Or maybe her silence had a more drastic significance: she no longer felt she could trust me; I'd let her down. She hadn't managed to convince me, to convert me to her faith, and now she wanted nothing more to do with me. I pictured her shut up in her flat, alone with her obsession, taking refuge in her perfect, familiar circle of fears. I went to my bedroom, switched on the television and checked the news channels, but none seemed to be reporting the fires yet. At two in the morning, exhausted, I turned out the light and slept until almost midday.

When I woke up I went straight down to the bar to read the papers. There was little more coverage than a fortnight ago and I wondered if I was the only one who was interested in the fires. There had in fact been three: two fairly close together in the district of Flores, at more or less the same time (the ones I'd seen from the plane), and another a little later in Montserrat. Again, all three fires were in furniture stores, and they had all been started in the same simple but effective way, with petrol poured under the door and a match. At least now there was a suspect: several witnesses claimed to have seen a Chinese man with a canister of petrol riding away from the scene on a bicycle. I looked in another newspaper. Here too it mentioned a man with oriental features. A separate article made the link with the fires of a fortnight ago and ventured a theory: the man could be working for the Chinese Mafia, setting fire to uninsured furniture stores, thus bankrupting the owners, who had to sell their premises off cheaply to oriental supermarket chains. I laid aside the newspaper with a mixture of astonishment and disbelief. Once again, I thought, local colour had defeated me: what chance did my group of incendiary artists stand against a Chinese on a bicycle? I thought, with a flicker of resistance, that I shouldn't let myself be cowed by Argentinian reality, that I should learn from the Master and overcome it, but mysteriously something inside me had given up as I read the articles.

The novel I'd planned to write now seemed silly and unsustainable and I wondered whether I shouldn't abandon the whole idea.

I spent the rest of the afternoon in a state of despondent lethargy, thinking of J much more often than I would have imagined. My kitchen cupboards and fridge were empty and as night fell I forced myself to go out and stock up for the week. When I got back I switched on the television again. This time the fires were in the news and the mysterious Chinese was the celebrity of the moment. On one channel they showed a rough identikit portrait and shots of the various burnt-out premises. On another they were interviewing the owners, who were shaking their heads sadly, pointing to smoke-blackened walls and furniture reduced to ashes. It all now seemed distant, unconnected to me, as if they were no longer *my* fires, as if reality had been skilfully manipulated to suit the cameras. I changed channels until I found a movie but fell asleep halfway through.

I was woken just before midnight by the insistent, painful stab of the telephone ringing. It was Luciana. She was screaming and it took me a moment to understand her. 'What have you got to say now?' she sobbed. 'This is what he was planning.' Eventually I grasped that she wanted me to switch on the television. Still holding the phone, I groped for the remote control. All the channels were showing the same news: a horrific fire had spread through an old people's home on the top floor of a building. The fire had started in an antique shop on the ground floor. 'The antique shop,' Luciana screamed. 'He set fire to the shop below the home.' The shop window had shattered and flames had engulfed a huge tree in the street outside. The trunk had acted as a wick, the fire running up and spreading to the upper floors of the building. Some of the branches were still in flames, touching the balconies. Firemen had managed to get inside but so far they'd brought out only dead bodies: many of the residents were bedridden and had been suffocated by the smoke.

'They called from the hospital – my grandmother's dead. I've got to go and identify the body because Valentina's still a minor. But I can't do it. I can't!' she screamed desperately. 'I can't cope with another morgue, the corpses, the undertakers. I don't want to see any more corpses. I can't go through it all again.' She started crying again, a devastated sobbing that seemed for a moment as if it might turn into a howl.

'I'll come with you,' I said. 'Look, this is what we're going to do.' I tried to sound practical and authoritative, like a parent talking to a frightened child. 'There's no hurry to identify the body, the main thing is for you to calm down. Take a pill now. Have you got some there?'

'Yes,' she said, between sobs. 'I already took one, before calling you.'

'Good. Now take another one, but only one, and wait for me to arrive. Don't do anything else. Turn off the TV and stay in bed. I'll be there as soon as I can.'

I asked if her sister was with her and her voice fell to a whisper.

'I told her. The day I saw you, after she came out of his house. I told her everything but she didn't believe me. I said Bruno hadn't believed me and now he was dead. She's just seen the fire on TV. She was with me when they called from the hospital, we watched them bringing out the bodies, but even now she doesn't believe me. She doesn't realise,' her voice faltered, terrified, 'she doesn't realise *she's next*.'

'Don't think about that now. Promise me you won't think about any of it until I get there. Just try to get some sleep.'

I hung up and sat for a few seconds, eyes riveted on the screen. They'd already brought out fourteen bodies and the count was still rising. I couldn't believe it either. It was, simply, too monstrous. On the other hand, weren't all these bodies the perfect screen? The name of Luciana's grandmother amongst a growing list of dead. No one would look into it as a separate case; her death would remain for ever invisible, merged with the general tragedy. This fire wouldn't even be considered arson, but an accident, a tragic side effect of the attacks on furniture stores. Maybe the Chinese man would be made to pay, that is if he really existed and they caught him. Was Kloster capable of planning and carrying out such an atrocity? Yes, at least in his novels he was. I could almost hear his contemptuous retort: 'So you want to send me to prison because of my books?'

Then I had the fatal, misguided impulse, which I have regretted every single day since – the urge to act, to *intervene*. I dialled Kloster's number. He didn't answer and there was no answering machine. I dressed quickly and hailed a taxi outside my building. We drove through the night, its silence interrupted only by the distant wail of fire engines. Over the radio in the taxi I heard news of more fires, multiplying like a virus across the city, and now and again the morbid repetition of the list of dead at the care home. The taxi dropped me outside Kloster's house. The windows were shuttered and I could see no light through the slats. I rang the doorbell a couple of times, to no avail. Then I remembered what Luciana had once said about Kloster and his habit of swimming in the evening. I went into the café where she and I had sat two weeks earlier, and asked the waiter if there was a club nearby with a swimming pool. There was, just round the block. I hurried there. Marble steps led up to a revolving door with a brass plaque beside it. Inside I rang the bell at the reception desk and

a tired-looking porter appeared. I asked for the swimming pool and he pointed to a sign showing the opening
hours: it closed at midnight. I described Kloster and
asked if he'd seen him. He nodded and indicated the
staircase leading up to the bar and the pool tables. I
went up the two flights and found myself in a large
smoke-filled room. A crowd of poker players sat in
silent concentration at round tables. They glanced up
warily when I appeared at the top of the stairs, but soon
went back to their cards. It was only then that I realised
why the club was still open at midnight: it was a thinly
disguised gambling den. At the bar a muted television
was tuned to a sports channel. There was a ping-pong
table, with the net already taken down, and, beyond it,
a few pool tables. At the last one, next to a window
looking on to the street, I saw Kloster, playing alone, a
glass resting on the edge of the table. I walked over. His
hair was swept back and still damp, as if he'd only just
come out of the changing room, and his sharp features
stood out in the lamplight. He was absorbed in calculating the trajectory of a ball, his chin resting on his cue,
and it was only when he moved to a corner of the table
and prepared to take his shot that he noticed me.

'What are you doing here? Some fieldwork on games
of chance? Or have you come for a game with the boys?'

He looked at me serenely with only mild interest as he
applied chalk to the tip of his cue.

'Actually I was looking for you. I thought you'd be at the pool, but they told me you were here.'

'I always come up here after my swim. Especially since discovering this game. I rather looked down on it when I was young. I thought it a game for bar-room show-offs – you know what I mean. But it has interesting metaphors, and its own little philosophy. Have you ever tried to play it seriously?'

I shook my head.

'Essentially it's geometry, of course. And the most classical kind: action and reaction. The kingdom of causality, you might say. Any spectator can see the obvious trajectory for a shot. That's how beginners play: thinking only about sinking the next ball, they pick the most direct path. But as soon as you start to understand the game you realise that what really matters is controlling the trajectory of the white *after* impact. And that's considerably more difficult. You have to anticipate all the possible ways the balls might strike one another, the chain reactions. Because the true object of the game, the trick, lies not in sinking the ball, but in sinking it and leaving the white free and positioned so that it can strike again. That's why, of all possible trajectories, professionals sometimes choose the least direct, the most unexpected, because they're always thinking one shot ahead. They want not just to strike the ball, but to strike and not stop until they've sunk them all. It's geometry, yes, but of a fierce kind.' He moved to where he'd left his glass, took a sip, and looked at me, eyebrows slightly raised. 'So what's the question that was so urgent you came all the way here and couldn't wait till morning?'

'You haven't heard about the fire? You don't know anything?' I scanned his face for any sign of pretence, but Kloster remained unperturbed, as if he really didn't know what I was talking about.

'I heard there were some fires yesterday, something about furniture showrooms. But I don't really keep up with the news,' he said.

'A couple of hours ago there was another one – an antique shop below a care home. The home Luciana's grandmother lived in. They're still bringing out the bodies. Luciana's grandmother was one of the first pronounced dead.'

Kloster seemed to take in the information gradually. He stood preoccupied for a moment, as if he were having trouble reconciling it with another train of thought. He laid the cue across the table and I thought I saw his hand shake slightly. He turned to me, his face sombre.

'How many dead?' he asked.

'They still don't know,' I said. 'They've found fourteen bodies so far. But it's likely several more will die in hospital overnight.'

Kloster nodded. He bowed his head and placed his hand over his face like a visor, pressing his temples.

Slowly he paced up and down alongside the table, eyes hidden by his hand. Was he feigning this emotion? He seemed to be genuinely affected by the news, but in a way I couldn't quite fathom. Eventually he looked up, his gaze distant so that he seemed to be talking to himself.

'A fire,' he said, still apparently struggling with his thoughts. 'Fire. Of course. And I can see now why you came all the way here.' He suddenly flashed me a contemptuous look. 'You think I left home a couple of hours ago with my swimming things, torched that care home, then came here to do my hundred lengths in perfect calm while the old folks burned to a crisp. That's what you think, isn't it?'

I shrugged doubtfully. 'Luciana saw you a couple of weeks ago, standing outside the home, staring up at the balconies. That's why she got in touch with me: she thought you were planning something against her grandmother.'

Kloster eyed me, still slightly contemptuous, but now seeming exasperated as well.

'That's possible. Quite possible. In my novel I had to plot a murder in an old people's home. I went to several, in different parts of town. I looked at some from outside, making mental notes. But in a couple of them I pretended I needed to put a relative in a home and looked round inside. You wouldn't believe how easy it is to get into those places. I was looking for distinctive features for a particularly ingenious murder. But I was only ever thinking of *one* murder, *one* person. Destroying the whole place – such a simple, brutal solution never occurred to me. I have to say, I'm surprised myself every time by the *method*. Though if you think about it, fire was an obvious choice.'

There was something distracted in the way he spoke now, as if he were addressing a third person. He looked at me, but his eyes darted about, and he started pacing again, as if engaged in a furious inner struggle.

'All those dead – they're innocent,' he said. 'This wasn't meant to happen. This definitely was not meant to happen. It's time to stop him. But it's too late. I wouldn't know how to.'

He came very close and his expression had changed again: he seemed now to want to show me his naked face, at my mercy, to be judged.

'I'll ask again: do you believe it was me? Do you believe it was me every time?'

I couldn't help stepping back. There was something ravaged and terrifying in Kloster's eyes. A much deeper, darker madness than Luciana's seemed to burn there.

'No, I don't,' I said. 'I no longer know what to believe.'

'Well, you should believe it,' said Kloster darkly. 'You should believe it, but for another reason. A few hours ago, before coming here, I started writing that very scene, the murder in the care home. I left a rough draft on my desk. And as you see, it's happened again. Only the method changes. As if he wanted to stamp his seal. Or make fun of me. A correction of *style*. It's happened every time. All I had to do was write. At first I tried to convince myself that they must be coincidences. Very strange coincidences, of course. Too precise. But the dictation . . . had already begun. I suppose you could say it's a work in collaboration.'

'In collaboration? With whom?'

Kloster looked at me warily, as if he might have gone too far and was suddenly unsure whether he should go on. Perhaps it was the first time he'd told anyone.

'I hinted at it, the first time we spoke, when I admitted that I didn't believe the deaths were occurring entirely by chance. But at the time I couldn't put it into words. It was the only possible explanation but also the one nobody would believe. Not even I fully believed it, until now. Perhaps you still won't. You may remember, I mentioned the preface to Henry James's *Notebooks*.'

'Yes, I remember it perfectly: you said that's where you got the idea of dictating your novels.'

'There's something else in the book. Something he reveals in some of the more personal notes, which I never would have suspected of the ironic and cosmopolitan Henry James. He had, or believed he had, a guiding spirit, or "guardian angel". Sometimes he calls him his "demon of patience", at others his "daimon", or the "blessed Genius", or "mon bon". He invokes him, waits for him, sometimes senses him sitting near. He says he can even feel his breath on his cheek. He entrusts himself to this spirit, appeals to him when inspiration fails, waits for him whenever he moves into a new study to write. A guiding spirit that was with him all his life, until he started dictating. This may be what most struck me in the *Notebooks*: all references to his angel ceased at the moment when another person entered his workroom, when spoken words replaced silent pleas. As if the secret collaboration had been ended for ever. I remember that when I read the invocations of the guardian angel I couldn't help smiling: I had trouble picturing venerable, distinguished Henry James pleading like a child to an invisible friend. It seemed puerile, if touching, and made me feel as if I'd been snooping and had seen something I shouldn't have. Yes, I found it laughable and I forgot about it almost immediately. Until I started dictating myself. But unlike James, it was through dictation that I had a visitation of my own. Only it wasn't a guardian angel.'

He took another sip from his glass and stared into the distance for a moment, before placing the glass back on the edge of the table and looking at me again with the same open expression.

'I think I've already told you about that morning: after days of silence, paralysis, I started dictating to Luciana again in a sudden rush, as if transported. As I was dictating to her, *someone else was dictating to me* in an imperious, brutal whisper that cut through all scruples, all doubts. I wanted the scene ahead of me, the scene at which I'd stopped, to be especially horrific. The bloody but methodical revenge carried out by the Cainites. I'd never written anything like it before; I'd always preferred more civilised, more discreet murders. I thought it wasn't in my nature, that I'd never be able to do it. But suddenly, all I had to do was *listen*. Listen to the dark, ferocious whisper that conjured up the knife and the throat with perfect realism. Follow the miraculous connection, the voice that wouldn't back down before anything, that killed and killed again. Thomas Mann said that, while writing *Death in Venice*, he had the sensation of moving forward unhindered, the impression, for the first time in his life, of being "carried in the air". I too felt it for the first time. But I can't say that the voice carrying me was benevolent. Instead it seemed to be dragging me, controlling me, a primitive, superior evil that I had to obey. A voice that I could only just follow, that had taken over everything, that seemed to wield the knife with savage joy, as if saying: "It's easy, it's simple, you do this and this and this." By the time I had finished dictating the scene I was surprised to find that I didn't have bloody hands. But something of the almost sexual euphoria, of the fit of inspiration, persisted. A remnant of that all-powerful urge. I think it was this terrible combination that made me try to kiss Luciana. I only returned to reality when I realised she was resisting.'

He raised his head slightly and shook it almost imperceptibly, as if he were reproving himself and trying to shake off the memory.

'Later, that night, I reread the pages I had dictated to her. There was no doubt: they were someone else's. I could never have written anything like them, without error or hesitation. The language was primordial, with a terrible, primitive force that seemed to touch deep evil. I was terrified seeing the words there, fixed on paper, incontrovertible proof that it had been *real*. I couldn't work on the novel again; I felt it was fatally contaminated by that other writing. I stopped at the last sentence I had dictated to Luciana before she got up to make coffee. I put it away in a drawer and tried to forget about it, to deny what had happened with rational arguments. Then the series of tragedies: I lost my daughter, I lost my life. I was disconnected from the world, devoid of thought. All I could do was watch the film of Pauli, over and over. I thought I'd never write again. Until, that summer, I went to the beach at Villa Gesell, and saw that body disappear out to sea. It was like a sign written in the water. Anyone would say it was an accident, and that's what I thought at the time. But I understood what the sign was telling me. I knew the story I had to write. I didn't know, I never could have imagined, that it was his novel – the beginning of his novel. I returned to Buenos Aires the next day: I just wanted to get started. Suddenly everything seemed clear. I could see the tiny but unmistakable light at the end of the tunnel – the subject of the novel. After all, it wasn't so different from the story about the Cainites that I'd set aside. Only this one would take place in the present day. There'd be a girl, rather like Luciana. And someone who'd lost a daughter, like me. The girl would have a family just like Luciana's. For once in a novel I wanted to keep some resemblance to real life, because I felt that the secret source, the wound I needed to prod, was my own. I didn't want to forget myself, to let myself be swept along, as in my other books, by the flow of my imagination. The subject, of course, was punishment – what constitutes proportionate punishment. An eye for an eye, states the *lex talionis*. But what if one eye is smaller than the other? I had lost a daughter, but Luciana didn't have any children. Yet my grief cried out that a daughter wasn't equivalent to a short-term boyfriend with whom Luciana didn't even seem to get on. I began writing with rigorous determination, but something seemed to have dried up, died inside me, as if my daughter's death meant I was banished not only from the human race, but from my own writing. The few lines I managed to scribble each day were unrecognisable. Nothing was right. So, in my own way, I invoked him. I appealed to him night after night, until suddenly I realised I was no longer alone. He had returned. I could feel him once again at my shoulder. And I let him do as he pleased – I let him dictate to me again. He provided the momentum, gave the command, made the tuning fork hum. It was like a gradual thaw, as if the stone I had become had started to ooze. But I was writing again, and I knew exactly to whom I owed it. Inwardly I referred to him as my "Sredni Vashtar". He was invisible, but his monstrous voice was as familiar as the sound of a loved one's breathing. He was not only real but almost palpable, and I was sure anyone would know which sentences on the page were his. At first, it was almost all of them. But the physical act of writing, like a magical exercise of the muscles, gradually brought back my old skill, some of my old self. He'd made the electricity flow, made the dead man live again. I came back to life. I recovered my old pride, the only one I have, and no longer wanted his company. I went back to my long vigils, to my usual wavering and meandering, to my own imagination. But it wasn't easy to get rid of him. I could feel him riding on my shoulders, like the Old Man of the Sea. And of course his sentences were always better than mine – primordial, savage, direct. But I managed to reject them one by one, despite the temptation. Eventually I felt I was alone again. And I thought I was free of him at last.'

'When was this?'

'Almost a year later, just before writing the scene with the parents' death. I pictured them dying at their house by the beach, during their winter holiday, from a carbon monoxide leak from the boiler. That kind of accident happens every year. I didn't consider any other possibility. When I went back to writing on my own, I realised that some of my bitterness had gone, life had resumed, and I was starting to forget Luciana. The novel was no longer a voodoo doll. My writing had drifted in another direction. The parents in the novel were no longer Luciana's parents. I could view them artistically and devise the kind of death that best suited them, just like characters in any of my novels. After all, I'd spent a lifetime thinking up murders. So perhaps because I no longer had the same desire for revenge, I imagined a painless end for them, in their sleep, together in the marital bed. I wrote the scene with absolute calmness of spirit. Then, a couple of weeks later, I received Luciana's letter: her parents *really had died*. The letter was muddled – really she was begging me to forgive her for suing me, which was what had started it all, but she mentioned her parents' death as if it were something I would know. And she told me the date of

their death: *it was the day after I had written the scene.*
Of course, I was stunned. I looked for news of the case in
the papers. All the details were there. The circumstances
were slightly different, but it seemed only to be a difference of style: a much more horrible death but, in its way,
natural.'

'When you say *natural*,' I broke in, suddenly remembering what I had thought, what I'd felt I'd glimpsed, in
the basement of the newspaper offices, 'do you mean . . .'

'In the most literal sense. There were no boilers or
ovens involved, nothing that had anything to do with
civilisation. Poison from a plant – a simple, primitive
death. I realised immediately that he had devised it. And
as you'll understand, I was shocked. It was one thing
sensing his presence in the whispering, in the strange
communion of that private dictation or in the blameless
lines of a text, but quite another admitting that he
existed outside me and could kill in the real world. I
didn't take that step. Though the evidence was there
before my eyes, I couldn't believe that there was a causal
connection, that reality had responded to my text. Those
past few months, as I said, I had come to feel like myself
again. The few lines I managed to set down laboriously
every day had gradually restored me to my former self.
And my former self had always been sceptical, even contemptuous, of the irrational. I had, after all, studied
science at university, and had written entire passages

mocking the very idea of religion. I decided to consider the dictation episode as a passing fit, a period of mental disturbance brought on by the loss of my daughter. This was something I could admit: grief had made me temporarily lose my mind. Even so, even though I refused to believe, I was a little shaken, so I left the novel at that point. It remained in a drawer for years. It wasn't exactly a superstitious fear that I felt, but something more personal: the secret motor, my desire for revenge, had subsided. With the death of Luciana's parents I had, at last, however monstrous this may sound, achieved reparation. My wound had healed, my flame had died down and, after the first moment of astonishment at the coincidence, I was at peace, if a little guilty, because I couldn't help feeling that in anticipating and preparing those deaths in my imagination I had, in a mysterious, indirect way, prompted them. In any case, the ratio now seemed right and I almost wrote back to Luciana. Truly I no longer bore her any ill will.'

'But at some point you reopened that drawer.'

Kloster nodded slowly. 'Years passed – three, four, I forget how many. I didn't think about any of it again, and in the meantime wrote other books. Until one day I read a short article in the paper about premonitions in dreams. You know what I mean: one night someone dreams about the death of a loved one and the next day it comes true, as if the dream were really a prediction, an arrow shot at the target. The article was written by a professor of statistics, and the tone was rather mocking. He did a simple sum calculating the probabilities and showed that the likelihood of a premonition in a dream coming true was very low, but not so low that, in a big city like Tokyo or Buenos Aires, the coincidence between two events – person X having the dream and their loved one Y dying – didn't routinely occur. Of course to the person who has the dream the coincidence is astonishing and they see it as a psychic phenomenon, the manifestation of a supernatural power; but for someone who could look down on an entire city at night and keep count of everyone's dreams, it would be no more surprising than a bingo-caller hearing someone shout out "Bingo". The article was very persuasive and made me think differently about the scene I'd written and the death of Luciana's parents. I was rather ashamed of having given in to the fundamentally arrogant and superstitious belief that my writing could have had such an effect on reality. With hindsight, it seemed obvious that it had simply been a coincidence between two unrelated events. That night there must have been an army of writers imagining, as I was, some death or other. It just happened that what I'd imagined subsequently took place. A lottery number in a sea of statistics, assigned to me by chance. I opened the drawer again and reread the novel to where I'd left it. But now I was surprised by something else: it was the best thing I'd ever written. And, stranger still, I couldn't distinguish between his writing and mine. I could no longer point out which sentences had been dictated to me. The whole text seemed to be both familiar and written by someone else. This had happened before when I'd gone back to some of my books and found passages I didn't recognise, but what I'm trying to say is that I decided to believe – wanted to believe – that it was me who had written every one of those pages. That all the ideas were mine alone. I wanted to *take possession* of the book. But really I should say that it took possession of me once again. I couldn't resist continuing. I realised that there was no doubt it would be my masterpiece, perhaps my only great novel. So you see, I gave in to that other arrogant superstition: wanting to create something "great". Anyway, I returned to it, night after night. Until the time came to imagine the brother's death.'

'Even when you knew what might happen?'

'In the novel, the process of revenge had to continue,' said Kloster, as if it were too late for regrets. 'But I did waver. I had months of doubts, of scruples. As in De Quincey's tale, I felt the thin line, on the edge of the abyss, between dabbling in murder and becoming a fully fledged murderer. Then I thought I'd found a solution. But I was wrong. I thought if I simply devised a highly improbable death, a set of extreme coincidences, it wouldn't be replicated in real life. Luciana had once mentioned that while he was at medical school her brother had been on a work placement in the prison service. It was the only thing I knew about him. In addition, I had, as you know, corresponded with a number of prisoners in different jails. I linked the two and imagined a convict in a high security prison pretending to have a seizure so as to be taken to the infirmary. Luciana's brother, now a junior doctor, would be on duty that night and the convict would stab and kill him while trying to escape. As I wrote the scene, I added a few details, from the little I knew about the inside of prisons, that would make the chain of events seem more believable, yet, subtly, more unlikely. But *it happened again*. Once again, in a slightly different way; once again, as if it were a version revised by someone bolder, crueller. And, as if it were part of the joke, in an even more bizarre sequence of events. The convict hadn't tried to escape: his own jailers had opened the door so he could leave to burgle people's houses. Luciana's brother no longer worked at the prison but during his time at the infirmary he'd met, of all the wives of all the prisoners, the wife of the most vicious. I first found out about it, as you did, as everybody did, in the papers. That morning I read, and reread in disbelief, the name of Luciana's brother. Same age, same profession, and from the photo I could see they looked very alike. Yes, it had happened again.'

'And once again there was something savage, primitive, about it,' I said, at last seeing the connection I'd missed. 'The man killed him with his bare hands, without using his gun.'

'Exactly. It bore his stamp, I could tell immediately. I was beginning to understand his methods, his preferences: the wild sea waves, the natural poison of fungi, the cruelty of one man attacking another like a beast with claws and teeth, as at the dawn of time. A few days later that policeman, Ramoneda, came to see me and showed me the anonymous letters. They were uncouth but precise, and effective. I almost told him everything, as I'm telling you now. But he had his own theory. He spotted a book by Poe on my bookshelves and started talking about *The Tell-Tale Heart*, of the desire to confess that he'd seen again and again in murderers. I realised from the way he spoke about Luciana that he suspected her. He asked if I had any samples of her handwriting. I gave him the letter she had sent me a few years earlier, in which she asked for forgiveness. He read it carefully and while he was comparing the handwriting he confided that Luciana had spent time in hospital, with a syndrome known as "morbid guilt". Sufferers secretly feel guilty about some harm they've done for which they haven't been punished. Indirectly, and in different ways, they seek to punish themselves. Ramoneda said Luciana was obsessed with the thought that she'd had something to do with my daughter's death. Hearing this, so many years later, caused me a sort of belated, bitter joy. I'd wanted her to have to think of Pauli every day of her life, and that wish had also been granted. Ramoneda said nothing more and I was sure that, whatever his suspicions, he'd keep them to himself and not do anything. After all, he had his culprit and pressure from the entire government to close the case and hush up the scandal over the convict's escape.

'Once he'd left, though, I found myself wondering whether this wasn't another possible explanation. A rational explanation. I considered each death again in this new light. Luciana could have put some substance in her boyfriend's coffee: she studied biology, she'd have known what to use that would go undetected in a postmortem and she was there with him every day. And the following year, Luciana could have planted poisonous fungi in the little wood, during the same kind of lightning visit to Villa Gesell that she accused me of. Wasn't she the one who knew all there was to know about fungi? And finally, Luciana could have written the anonymous letters. She probably knew about her brother's relationship with that woman. But I had to dismiss this possibility before it went very far: Luciana could never have achieved the insane synchronicity between the dates of the deaths and the progress of my novel.

'Even so, considering another hypothesis, one that

came, unexpectedly, from an outside source, made me regain hope that there was room for a rational explanation, even if I couldn't come up with one. As you see, there was still something stubborn in me. I couldn't accept, intellectually, that what had already occurred twice might occur again. So I set out to challenge him. I proceeded like a sceptic who deliberately walks under a ladder. I decided to write one more death, *to test him*. The scientific test of repetition. At least that was how I justified it to myself at the time, but I know there was something else. I don't mind admitting it now: I didn't want to stop writing the novel, even though I knew another person might die as a result. Even knowing this, I couldn't resist. So I started devising the next death. As I said earlier, I visited several care homes and considered several ingenious variants. What I really wanted was a murder that was the opposite of his style. That was *antithetical* to all that he was. Strangely, it was you who gave me the idea, when we spoke about Luciana's grandmother and you said that it wouldn't count against me if she died a natural death. As soon as you'd said it, I knew that's what it had to be. It was simple, perfect – a natural death. And to a certain extent it left me with a clean conscience. I wouldn't be imagining and writing a murder, but a merciful release for someone who'd been bedridden for years. This afternoon I made up my mind at last to write the first draft. *One* death. *One* person.

That's all I wanted. Do you believe this at least?' Kloster looked me straight in the eye, as if expecting an immediate answer.

'It doesn't matter what I believe,' I said. 'What matters is what Luciana believes. She called me this evening, after the fire. That's why I'm here. She's desperate, on the brink of madness, I think. I promised I'd go to see her. But I'd like you to come with me.'

'Me?' Kloster made a face, as if the very idea were distasteful. 'I don't see how it would help. I think it might even make things worse.'

'I want her to hear from you what you've just told me. Even only this small part of it: that since her parents' death, you no longer bear her any ill will. I think that, coming from you, would change everything for her.'

'And then we'd give each other a big Christian hug of reconciliation? That's rather naive of you, young man. Don't you see it no longer depends on me? Ten years ago, when I was in despair, my atheism faltered and I prayed. I prayed every night to a dark, unknown god. My prayer was heard and is slowly being answered. It came from me, but I can't now take it back. Because the punishment, the full punishment, has already been written. *It is written.*'

'How do you know how much of it has been written? How do you know that a gesture of forgiveness now wouldn't change everything? If what you've told me is taking place as you say, there is one fundamental thing you could do: stop writing. Give it up right now.'

'I could even burn it, but there's no guarantee it would stop anything. It's outside me. And I think he's getting *ahead* of me now: this time he didn't wait for the scene to be fully written and finished.'

'So are you saying you refuse to come with me?'

'On the contrary: I said I'd like to stop it, if only I knew how. I'm prepared to try anything you say. But I'm sceptical about the results. We don't even know if she'd be willing to see me again face to face.'

'Why don't we ask her? Is there a phone here I can use?'

Kloster indicated the bar and signalled to the barman to let me use the telephone. Reluctantly the barman reached for an old Bakelite phone with a thick spiral cord. I took it to one end of the bar and dialled Luciana's number, waiting patiently for the dial to return between digits. A sleepy voice answered.

'Luciana?'

'No, it's Valentina. Luciana's gone to bed. But she said to wake her if you called.'

There was a click on the line, as the receiver was lifted in another room, and I heard Luciana's voice, weak and defeated.

'You said you'd come,' she said, only faint reproach in her voice, as if it no longer surprised her to be let down. 'I was waiting for you, because I . . .' Her voice faded to a whisper and she said, as if she had remained stuck at this one thought: 'I can't deal with the coffin.'

'I'm here with Kloster,' I said. 'I want to bring him with me, so you can hear what he has to say.'

'Bring *Kloster*? Here? Now?' In her disbelief, she seemed unable to comprehend the meaning of my words. Or rather, I thought I perceived something helpless and disoriented in her voice, as if she could no longer think coherently and so clung to these questions, before letting them slip from her grasp. Suddenly she laughed bitterly, and for a moment sounded lucid again. 'Yes, why not? We can have a chat, the three of us, like old friends. Isn't it funny? The first time I went to see you I still thought there was a slight hope that I could convince you. I had a plan, something I'd been thinking of doing for years. I just needed your help. I learned from him. I'd planned it all down to the last detail. I thought I could pre-empt it, before it was too late. *I didn't want to die*,' she said, pitifully, and she started crying quietly. A moment passed before she spoke, her voice reproachful again: 'The only thing I never thought, never could have imagined, was that you would believe *him*.'

'I don't believe him,' I said. 'I don't know what to believe. But I think you should listen to what he has to say. If only for a moment.'

There was a long silence, as if Luciana was weighing

the implications and dangers of the visit, or for once was seeing everything from another perspective.

'Why not?' she said again, but now she seemed strangely detached, indifferent, as if nothing could touch her any more. Or perhaps (but I only realised this later) she suddenly had a new plan, one in which she no longer needed me, and her sudden acceptance, the unexpected meekness, was her way of setting it in motion. 'We can face each other again. Like civilised people. I suppose I'm curious to find out how he convinced you.'

'It would only take a moment. And afterwards I'll go and sort out the coffin.'

'You'll sort it out? You'd do that for me?' Her tone suddenly switched to gratitude, so that she sounded like a little girl thankful for a huge, unexpected favour.

'Of course I would. You need to rest.'

'To rest,' she said longingly. 'Yes. I'm so tired.' She seemed to drift for a moment, lost in her dark thoughts. 'But there's Valentina. It's too dangerous for me to go back to sleep – I have to protect Valentina. I'm the only one who can protect her.'

'Nothing's going to happen to Valentina,' I said, aware of the dishonesty and weakness of the attempt to reassure her. Too much had happened since the last time I'd said something similar.

'I don't want him to see her,' she whispered. 'I don't want her to see him again.'

'I'll be there,' I said. 'And there's no reason for him to see her.'

'I know what he wants. I know why he's coming here,' she said, madness in her voice again. 'But I want Valentina to be saved, at least.'

'I've got to go now,' I said, keen to end the conversation. I was afraid she'd change her mind. 'We'll be there in ten minutes.'

I hung up and signalled to Kloster that she had agreed. He leaned his cue carefully against the wall and followed me to the stairs without a word.

12

I now come to the most difficult part of my story. I've tried many times since to return in memory to those moments, beginning when Kloster and I left the club. I've gone over the scenes many times, as if they were stills from a movie, searching for something that might have foretold what I failed to see until it was too late. But though I later examined them from all angles, those few, fatal events didn't yield any clues. Kloster was plunged in hostile silence, as if he were being forced against his will to perform an unpleasant duty. We got into a taxi with a loud radio and I gave the driver Luciana's address. The man warned he'd have to take a roundabout route as some streets were blocked off because of the fires. Although neither of us had asked, he told us the Chinese man had been caught, in a raid in the Bajo Flores district, and that a map marked with the locations of over a hundred more furniture stores had been found in his house. Despite this, he said, there had been more fires that night. Bored thugs, pyromaniacs, rival shop owners taking advantage of the chaos to settle scores, who could tell? He spoke out of the corner of his mouth, head turned slightly, appearing to address Kloster rather than me. But Kloster gave no sign that he was listening. At the first intersection there were barriers and a policeman was diverting traffic. The taxi driver pointed out the fire engines further down the street and the blackened façade of a building from which dark smoke billowed in the light of the street lamps. I asked if anyone else had died in the fires and he shook his head. The only dead were the residents of the old people's home. Some of them were strapped to their beds, he added, so they hadn't been able to get out. Nearly all of them had died: that was the real tragedy. I glanced at Kloster, but he remained expressionless, as if he hadn't heard a word. He was tapping his foot impatiently on the taxi's rubber mat. I detected no emotion in his face, but maybe he was just absorbed in his own thoughts. Every so often he looked out of the window at the street names, as if looking for a sign that the journey would soon be over.

At last we drew up outside Luciana's building. Kloster got out of the taxi first and walked hesitantly to the entrance. I followed and rang the bell for the top floor flat. In the deep night-time silence we heard a window open far above us and someone briefly leaned out. Then a voice came from the intercom but I couldn't tell if it was Luciana or her sister. Kloster and I waited without speaking. We could just hear, muffled by the glass door, the sound of the lift as it descended. The lift opened and, for a split second, as a figure approached, holding keys, head slightly bowed, I thought I was seeing an apparition: the perfect, recovered image of Luciana, exactly as she was at eighteen. She wore a long woollen coat that showed little of her body, but in the tall slim girl coming towards us I recognised the same upright, determined demeanour. And as she pushed back her hair to peer at the keys, I saw in a dizzying instant that her features reproduced, in a replica so perfect it seemed sacrilegious, the fresh face of Luciana as I had known her ten years earlier. The same high forehead, the same lively eyes, the parted lips. All of her was there suddenly before me, as if by a conjuring trick.

'My God, she looks exactly like Luciana!' I mumbled as she unlocked the door. I glanced at Kloster, as if I needed a witness to return me to reality. 'Like Luciana as she used to look,' I added involuntarily.

'Yes, the resemblance is extraordinary, isn't it? I was amazed too the first time I saw her,' said Kloster, and I wondered, as I stared at her with a fascination both old and new, whether he'd seen her again after that first time.

The only difference was that she looked even younger, even more radiant, than Luciana had at that age. But perhaps this was only because my eyes and I were now ten years older.

She opened the door and without hesitation, without fear, sought Kloster's eyes, as if there were some kind of secret understanding between them. She kissed him quickly on the cheek, then looked at me for the first time.

'My sister's talked about you a lot,' she said simply.

'How is she?' I asked.

'Calm. But that's what worries me – she's too calm. She's been sitting at the window since you called. She said you were both coming and that she was going to sit there to wait for you. After that she wouldn't say a word. She just got up to open the window when you rang the bell.'

As she spoke she'd opened the lift door and we now rose in silence. In the stillness of dawn, sounds were magnified and you could hear the screeching of pulleys and the metallic rumble of the lift as it climbed the echoing shaft. I couldn't get over my surprise as I stared at that face, now returned to me, and I experienced the attraction and emotion I'd once felt for those features all over again. Now that she wasn't speaking, the impression was even more intense and overwhelming. But she seemed only to have eyes for Kloster, though she was trying with teenage gaucheness not to show it. She'd obviously been crying but had put on a little make-up, and I sensed that if I hadn't been there she would already have been in Kloster's arms. Perhaps Luciana was right to fear for her after all. So why hadn't she made any excuse to get Valentina out of the house that evening? Why had she let her come down to open the door to us so that she was now standing opposite Kloster in the small lift? As I watched the floor numbers light up one after another I remembered that just now, on the phone, Luciana had alluded to her plan to kill Kloster. I'd dismissed it almost without taking it in but perhaps, as a last resort in her madness, she really did intend to kill him, and her unexpected agreement to my suggestion had been a way of getting him to the apartment. Perhaps right now, as her sister let us in, she was preparing her weapon. I thought all of this and discounted it once again, dismissing it as far-fetched and melodramatic. But I never contemplated, never *glimpsed* the other, yet more terrible, possibility that awaited us.

The lift stopped and as we emerged on to the small landing we heard the scream, a scream that still wakes me in the night: the hollow, terrified scream of someone leaping into the void. And before Valentina could unlock the front door, we heard the awful sound of the body hitting the ground. We rushed into the apartment. The window was wide open. We looked out and saw Luciana's broken body on the pavement below. She lay face down, in the ghostly light of the street lamps, her neck at a strange angle, as if it were the first thing to have been broken. She was quite motionless and a pool of blood was spreading from her side. I heard the scream, followed by despairing sobs, of Luciana's sister as she ran downstairs. Kloster and I were alone. I moved away from the window, because I couldn't look any more, and saw that Luciana had left a note pinned to the door. My hands were shaking violently, as if they didn't belong to me, but somehow I managed to take it down. *At least let her be saved*, she'd scrawled. Was it a message addressed to me, or a final plea to Kloster? He was still at the window and when he looked at me at last I could find no horror or sorrow on his face, no hint of compassion for another human being, but something I can only describe as admiration and awe, as if he were witnessing the work of a more powerful artist.

'Do you see?' he whispered. 'It's him again, absolutely. What could be simpler, more basic, more his style? A cosmic principle.' And he parted thumb and forefinger, as if releasing a particle into the void. 'Do you see?' he said again. '*The law of gravity.*'

Epilogue

I saw Kloster once more, at Luciana's funeral. It was one of those cold, luminous mornings in the city at the end of August when buds on the pollarded trees and lighter, more fragrant air hint at the arrival of spring. I overcame my long-standing aversion to funerals and made myself enter the citadel of terrifying, neat graves and time-worn vaults. If I was there, forcing myself to walk through the sea of stone crosses, it wasn't because of any debt I felt I owed Luciana, or to assuage my guilt – which the sight of her square of earth would only intensify – but because I wanted one last answer, or rather the painful confirmation of something I still couldn't quite believe.

Yet I had seen it happening before my eyes. I had seen it in Valentina's expression as she looked at Kloster in the lift, but I had failed to put two and two together. I'd chosen to believe that it was simply platonic admiration from reading his books, a teenage crush that Kloster wouldn't dream of reciprocating. But afterwards, in the chaos that followed Luciana's death, I had seen the speed and energy with which he had acted. I had watched him calm and console Valentina with what looked very much like an embrace, and organise things so that after giving my statement I had found myself heading home in a taxi, still stunned, while he took charge of everything, especially her. And I didn't protest, didn't raise any objections, because I could tell from Valentina's devastated face, behind her anguished tears, that this was what she wanted: to be alone with him.

I was at the cemetery in search of the final proof and I don't mind admitting that I hoped to find Valentina there alone. As I went over the events of that terrible night in my mind, despite all the evidence I believed there was still a remote hope that she had leaned on Kloster at that tragic moment because she was dazed and grief-stricken and he had seemed like a father figure. I kept telling myself that as soon as she had a chance to think, to reflect, she would push him away in horror.

But when, having made my way round the cremato-rium, I found the path to the newest graves, they were there together, she with her head bowed as if in prayer, he with a hand on her shoulder. There was no one else at the funeral. A solitary bunch of flowers lay on the patch of earth, still without a gravestone. In the silent cemetery they looked like a father and daughter now alone in the world. As I approached, Valentina looked up and something in her shrank back, as if she would have preferred not to see me. I could only think I reminded her of her sister's warnings against the person to whom she had entrusted herself. I approached anyway and offered her my condolences, obliging Kloster to remove his hand from her shoulder. I greeted him coldly and for a long while the three of us stood in awkward silence, staring at the flowers on the dark, freshly dug earth. I felt Kloster touch my elbow and signal for me to follow him. We moved a little distance away and he stopped and turned. He didn't show any anxiety, sorrow or remorse, merely a hint of curiosity, as if he wanted to clear up one last intriguing detail.

'There's something I never found out,' he said. 'Luciana left a note, didn't she? A message, which you kept.'

'Which I handed to the police,' I said. But Kloster didn't seem to register the intention behind my tone.

'So what did it say?'

'*At least let her be saved,*' I said.

For a moment Kloster was silent, as if he were repeating the words to himself in search of a deeper meaning and somehow approved of them.

'Though this was madness, yet there was method in 't,' he said. 'She tried to protect her sister to the end. Poor girl, she couldn't have been more wrong. How could she think I'd hurt Valentina when she's the one person for whom I've been able to feel anything since Pauli died. The one who's brought me back to life. Look around,' he said, waving an arm at the fields of crosses and headstones, the rows of graves stretching into the distance. 'This is the landscape I visited every day. *All green shall perish.* That's easier to believe here than anywhere else. But if you come here often enough, you see that moss eventually grows on the tombstones. So you see, I thought I was dead, dead like everyone here, but in spite of everything there was hope for me too.' He turned to look at Valentina with admiration. 'She's an extraordinary little person,' he said. 'Truly brave: she wouldn't believe anything her sister said about me.'

'But she's only seventeen,' I couldn't help saying. 'At that age, courage can be foolishness.'

'She is indeed only seventeen,' he said. 'Doesn't that make it doubly miraculous that she's become attached to me? The age difference doesn't seem to bother her. I hope it doesn't bother you.' He looked at me with a gleam of defiance but immediately reverted to a more benign manner. 'We've got something very powerful in common: she lost her father, I lost my daughter.'

'She lost *her whole family*,' I said, shaking with indignation, but Kloster hardly seemed to notice, as if what I'd said was trivial.

'We've both lost far too much,' he said. 'That's why I want to protect her more than anything. So that she can start a new life. When all this is over she's coming to live with me.'

'I hope it'll be a while before it's all over: there's going to be an investigation.'

'There's going to be an investigation?' echoed Kloster, as if he didn't really believe it, his tone almost mocking. 'Because of that obscure message, which seems to be one more sign of madness? It's quite clear what happened; I don't think there's any more to it. All three of us saw and heard the same. She wasn't pushed.'

'You knew, didn't you? When you pretended to let me convince you to see her. When you agreed to come with me. You knew she wouldn't be able to cope with seeing you.'

'You're giving me too much credit. How could I have *known* something like that? I had a feeling it would make things worse, and I said so. Maybe I should have been firmer. But by then I'd lost all will. I let myself be led. I realised it wasn't me writing the story, but someone ahead of me.'

'That's enough! I didn't believe you, not even the first time. It was you. You. Every time.'

My voice had grown louder and louder and I was now jabbing my finger into his chest. I was shaking with impotent rage. Realising that Valentina had turned to look, I lowered my finger slowly.

'Be careful, young man,' said Kloster coldly. 'You're starting to sound like Luciana. I'll tell you one last time.'

When I met his eyes, I saw that he was strangely serene, impassive.

'I'm not trying to get you to believe something I myself found so hard to believe, indeed that I only believe sometimes. But at least believe this: the only thing I've done, all these years, is set words down on paper.'

'You knew she'd reached the end of the line,' I insisted. 'You knew she was desperate and wouldn't be able to cope with seeing you face to face.'

'It was you who made me come with you, with your stupid idea of reconciliation,' said Kloster harshly, running out of patience.

We stared at each other in silence.

'Even if there's no investigation,' I said slowly, 'I'm going to make sure I write about it all. Every one of the deaths. Everything Luciana told me. Someone has to hear it.'

'I'm all in favour of novelists writing novels,' said Kloster. 'I could almost say I'm interested to see how the champion of randomness manages to turn me into the Great Demiurge – he who drowns swimmers without touching them and spreads poisonous spores in the woods and frees murderers from prison and sets fire to cities. And can even make people commit suicide with his telepathic powers! You'll turn me into a superman rather than a murderer. Come now, you know very well you won't be able to write about this without making a fool of yourself.'

'Maybe. But I'm still going to write about it and get it published. I owe it to Luciana. And maybe it will help protect her,' I said, glancing in Valentina's direction. Kloster followed my eyes.

'She doesn't need protecting,' he said. 'She might look very much like Luciana, but thankfully there are differences.'

The air was growing warmer in the morning sun and Valentina took off her coat. As Kloster spoke, my eyes fell instinctively on the small but pronounced curve of her breasts, taut and firm beneath a tight sweater. Could this be what Kloster was referring to? It did indeed look as if nature had taken this second chance, adding the missing brushstroke in the crucial place. I turned to see if I could tell from Kloster's face whether this was what he meant. But his expression was of another kind, and he might just as easily have been a proud father looking at his beautiful daughter, or a man in thrall to his new love. At any rate, at that moment, when he dropped his guard, the only thing I could tell for certain was that Kloster really did seem to love the girl. Not wanting to fall into this new trap, I reminded myself that all the monsters in history have kept a place and person for their tender feelings. Still, without even trying, he'd done it again: he'd made me *doubt*.

'I suppose I can't stop you writing what you want. But in that case maybe I'll finish my own manuscript, my version of the story. I'm only sorry that everyone will think it's inspired by events. That the events took place first. Cause and effect. Only you and I will know that it was the other way round.'

He looked up, as if already picturing it completed, at the tall trees bordering the cemetery, the translucent cloudless sky, and back to the girl waiting for him by the grave.

'It'll be unlike anything I've ever written before. I don't know about your novel,' he said, 'but mine will have a happy ending.'

Acknowledgements

To Carmen Pinilla, for her friendship, enthusiasm and faith in me. Without her constant encouragement, I wouldn't have reached the end.

To Dr Norberto García and Dr Carlos Presman, for their advice on forensic medicine.

To the lawyers (and writers) Hugo Acciarri and Gabriel Bellomo, for invaluable conversations about justice and proportionate punishment through the ages.

To the Civitella Ranieri Foundation, for an unforgettable residency in Italy, where part of this novel was written.

And to Marisol, for everything, and for her patient reading and re-reading.